BROKEN SPARROW

By

Raj Sinha

Become
Shakespeare
.com

First published in 2017 by

Becomeshakespeare.com
Wordit Content Design & Editing Services Pvt Ltd
Unit - 26, Building A-1, Nr Wadala RTO,
Wadala (East),
Mumbai 400037, India
T:+91 8080226699

©
ISBN : 978-93-86487-09-4

Contents

Acknowledgement

In memory of the dusty house on Exhibition Road in Patna where I was born

&

With gratitude to

The man in the blue checked shirt who started it all,

My brother Yashi for being my benevolent editor,

Suchi and Sudhanshu Shekhar for actually gifting me with a printed collection of my stories,

Mansi Singh for walking tall with me in a city full of snipers,

Ishan and Anshuman for their constant encouragement and creative inputs

Poonam for filling the voids with the softest of footfalls and

My many friends for reading my stuff and reverting with such kind words of appreciation and encouragement.

Dedication

To the five elders under whose watchful eyes I grew up discovering sunshine even when it rained.

THE FALTERING NAWAB

Down the river, up the stairs,
You'll find a garden lit with chairs,
They're white and deep, made from cane...
Boyhood memories, free of stain.

In my mind, the Bankipore Club will forever be bathed in sunshine and lit by the stars. It's a wonder because it is not as if I spent a great deal of my time there. In fact no one from the family did. *Papa* was an active member for sure and may even have been on its managing committee for some years, but he was not whiling away his life there even when he had his elder brother taking care of things – not by a long shot. Yet a lot happened at the Bankipore Club which keeps coming back to me, much like the waves from the Ganga that would keep lapping against the slanted embankment over which the Club was situated so picturesquely. There was even a gated flight of stone steps leading down to the river but since the water was quite deep even at the edge, the gate was always securely locked. Once however a motor launch had berthed there. I have a picture in my mind of looking down through the railings and seeking my parents in the group of happy people returning from that singular river-cruise and disembarking……….

And so the Club has remained with me like a shiny thing- it's almost as if I have held on to one of the coins I used to filch from my father's coat-pocket to buy sweets with.

Girish *Chacha*, England returned, young, incredibly handsome and single, was home on his annual leave from Calcutta. One evening *Papa*, the ever indulgent elder brother (in the footsteps of his own elder brother), took him to the Club.

Allow me to digress a bit here and give you a trivial insight into the community I hail from. I am a *kayastha* and among other things, *kayasthas* are known for their love of meat and drink. Generally speaking, we may not be affluent but we eat well and we are supposed to like our drink! This last so-called trait was extremely well balanced amongst *Dadi's* four sons. (Come to think of it, we were such a balanced family – it defined us and set us apart in so many ways.)

Babuji was a very moderate drinker. He hardly ever drank and when he did, it was to oblige an occasion or a friend. *Papa* was a regular drinker, but no matter how much he drank, he never got drunk. In fact this talent of his got so famously established, that it became a thing with his friends to get him drunk - somehow, sometime, somewhere. They never succeeded. Girish *Chacha* too was a "social" drinker but perhaps a little more intrepid than *Babuji*. Ram *Chacha* was in the Air Force and so I need say nothing more!

As I was saying, *Papa* took Girish *Chacha* to the Club that evening. He introduced him around and quickly enough, everyone was having a jolly good time. The Club was in fact a very jolly good place to go to. It was summer time so I suppose *Papa*, his friends and Girish *Chacha* were sitting around one of the many cane tables in the lush garden overlooking the quietly flowing Ganga. Booze and brotherhood were flowing with equal speed and Girish *Chacha* was soon discovering that whiskey was better confronted than handled with care! One round followed another and in no time at all he got to feel that he had not one but several brothers sitting around the table.

Presently, he eyed the river in the near distance and excellent swimmer that he was, contemplated crossing it. He was about to reveal his plans to *Papa* (who was happily signing for another round of drinks) when a distinguished looking man, clad in *chooridars* and *achkan,* walked up to their table with a smile and cigar on his lips. Everyone got up - everyone except Girish *Chacha*, that is. It would have been obvious to any onlooker that the elderly gentleman was someone highly regarded by the group of young men who were scrambling up from their chairs and welcoming him. The aristocratic looking man beamed around and spoke words of greeting with meticulous refinement. Someone plucked out a neighbouring chair and space was created to accommodate it. Just then *Papa* noticed that his younger brother was still sitting and eyeing the senior person with cold eyes.

"Girish, get up" he said urgently. So Girish *Chacha* got up and while doing so, picked up a cigarette and lighter from the table. He then proceeded to light up – it's worth noting that Girish *Chacha* was a non smoker. My father let these pulsating moments pass while keeping his eyes fixed on his brother. Finally, satisfied that all was in control, he looked at the elderly gentleman and said, "Sir, this is my younger brother Girish. He has come home on leave." He then turned with a very different expression to his brother and said, "And Girish, please meet Nawab *Saheb* of Usmansharif."

As the story goes, Girish *Chacha* continued to stare at the Nawab *Saheb* with cold eyes and raising his eye-brows archly asked, "Is that so?" He then blew smoke into the face of the fast dismantling nobility and still staring at the intruder, hissed, "*Bhaiya*, your Nawab *Saheb* means this to me." So saying he dropped the smoldering cigarette on the grass and stomped it to pulp with the toe-end of his brogues.

We were told that the blue-blooded Nawab *Saheb* withdrew from the scene with faltering grace while *Papa* picked up the shattered pieces as it were.

I can almost see him taking the glass from his younger brother's hand and putting it gently back on the table, then wrapping a protective yet firm arm around his shoulder, walking him to the railing overlooking the river and asking him if he would like to go home.....

Soon thereafter the brothers returned home. What happened next, I too was a witness to – Girish *Chacha* insisted that he would sleep on the floor of his mother's (*Dadi's*) verandah and that my father (who had a head of thick wavy hair those days,) was bald! *Dadi* kept administering motherly love on her son through the night while he kept stirring out of his stupefied state with a start every now and then and announcing, "*Bhaiya* you are bald." Even my father's exasperated admission that yes he was well and truly bald would not stop the brother from insisting that he was!

It was a night to remember. The good old Nawab Saheb of Usmansharif (who I suppose would have passed on by now), continues to live on. And why should he not? There must have been some jewel in his crown that he continues to shimmer like the twinkling stars that had smiled down on the lawns of my once beloved Bankipore Club, the night my father was ordained to go bald....

THE LAUGHING LEPER

In the steady monsoon drizzle,
Behold the Laughing Leper stands,
His begging bowl is on His head,
His ma tes, your children, shake His hands:
Your windows open to the sky,
unafraid and looking high...

A sk me what it is to feel isolated.

Sheel *Bhaiya* had *Bhaiya* for company.
Yashi had Vikram.

Even in family parlance it was common to hear "Harsh-Sheel" and "Vikram-Yashi" as one utterance. They moved in pairs, they shunned me in pairs and they ran away from me in pairs. I was not miserable or anything of the sort because for all such offshoots, my home still had such an immeasurable oneness about it. But I did feel isolated at times. I think *Dadi* was the first to sense this and so without any effort I became her *dulara* or the favored one. It was a good place to be in because *Amma* was a hard task master.

I, on the other hand, had a natural affinity for short cuts. Hence, from one perspective, I grew up between my mother and her mother-in-law. When things went really bad for me – example, a stinging slap on my cheek – I would go running to *Dadi* with *Amma* hot on my heels. On seeing me in my safe-zone and (to her absolute horror) discovering that now I was also crying, *Amma* would come to an abrupt halt, listen wordlessly to a shocked grand-mother and walk away. I would thus survive for the day and that is all that mattered.

But these were but mere, minor and sporadic skirmishes when compared to the one battle that I could never win.

School.

I might go to the extent of stating that I hated school even more than I loved my home and there can be no greater indictment in my book of judgment.

My first school was an all girls' school called St. Joseph's Convent (which took in boys too but only in kindergarten) and the hatred began on the very first day in the Blue Bus which I was made to board. There was a girl called Arati. She boarded the bus five hundred yards down the road from my house. On finding a "new boy" crying, she wet her cruel lips and made me her torture toy there and then and retained me as one throughout the time I attended that school.

Of the one year I spent at the Convent, I remember just two happy things. Mother Magda (the first woman I fell in love with) and the knowledge (useless though it was) that I was an angel. Mother Magda had installed a dainty little miniature barn in one corner of the classroom, and inside it a daintier little Jesus and Mary. Colorful toffee wrappers (representing each of us in the class) were given imaginative shapes and made to move, at the end of each day, in and around the barn according to our behavior. The nearer you were to Jesus and Mary the better you were supposed to be! Furthermore, all those who were represented inside the barn were given the ultimate prefix of 'angel'. Sweet Mother Magda thought I was an angel right from the start and I remained close to her Jesus till the end!

One day the Mother Superior, who had no doubt heard of this innovative technique made a surprise visit to the class. She beamed around and made polite sounds. Then she spoke to each of the many 'angels' and patted their heads.

"Who is this?" she asked, prior to sweeping out of the classroom. She was pointing at a toffee-wrapper that was way out of the barn and easily the farthest away from the Lord.

Arati raised her hand instantly.

"Why are you there, my child?" asked the Mother Superior, her spectacles glinting. "Wouldn't you like to be an angel?"

"No!" answered that horrible bully, thrusting her chin out.

"Goodness gracious me," exclaimed the Mother Superior, "Isn't she the devil herself!"

To me, five year old "angel", all that Mother Magda's innovative technique did was to make me conscious of goodness and good behavior. What got through my impressionable mind was that God was kind and benevolent and that human beings should try and emulate Him; what got through was that God was spelt with a capital G and "His" pronouns were spelt with a capital H; and what got through was the melancholy of the beautiful and kind Mother Magda. I carried these things out of the convent and I have carried them with me ever since.

I always wanted to be "good" – but the fact was that at home I was not. I was full of mischief and pranks. We used to wear "Naughty Boy" shoes from Bata those days and by all definitions I was naughty from my shoes upwards. But there were inexplicable and sudden shifts in my persona – I wonder now if the elders or anyone at home picked up these shifts. They are clear as a pattern to me when I look back.

In my very first year in St. Xavier's (the "boys only" counterpart of St. Joseph's), *Bhaiya* (who along with Sheel *Bhaiya* was two years senior to me) won a prize. He was a regular topper and the prize he won that year for coming "1st" was a book called "The Three Dogs". I have only carried one memory of that slim book. On the back cover was the picture of just one dog, looking backwards but trotting away into the distance. The name of the book and the picture on its back had summed up the story for me and made me cry. That image of the solitary dog has remained and its recollection still depresses me, even more so now when so many of my loved ones have taken their leave.

On another occasion, from my perch in one cozy corner, even as all of us were happily gathered and chatting in the Drawing Room at our house on Exhibition Road, I suddenly got the insight that all this would come to an end one day – these people whom I loved so much, the furniture, the room where we sat, the house itself. Everything. Nothing would remain. I ran my eyes around my family and started crying. No one could understand what had happened. I was too small and inarticulate to explain. So I just kept crying.....Not knowing what to do or make of my misery, it was decided that I should be made to lie down. So *Amma* held me close and took me out of the room. Since nothing was the matter with me, she just sat next to me after tucking me in bed and read her novel (both my parents were voracious readers) while occasionally running her fingers through my hair. In no time at all I was supremely happy and content, not least for the fact that I had been spared the mandatory "homework hour" that night. I smiled into myself, reached for my mother's hand and all was well with the world.....I probably drifted into sleep like that.

This was the magic of my home - its hand of God. It touched us in many ways and it is of little wonder to me that our house on Exhibition Road was so full of sky and sunshine, even when it rained.

There used to be a snub-nosed leper those days. A more cheerful person we had never seen. He would come occasionally to our house with his begging bowl and on our (the children's) demand wear that bowl like a hat and perform a unique jig of his own. His gap-toothed laughing face always stayed with us till long after he and our handful of coins were gone.

MAN IN THE BLUE
CHECKED SHIRT

Bicycles leaned on ancient walls
With children who were blessed from birth,
And there came for them a shimmer-man,
With a watch in a blue checked shirt.

We were children, growing up in a joint family at Patna. We lived in a large house with a larger compound. There was the main house - a squat, single storied structure with many rooms, high ceilings, verandahs and a portico without a car – and there were a couple of out-houses with tiled roofs. There was a huge garage too. Since we did not have a car those days, the garage had become the dump site for broken furniture, discarded tools, strung-up card-board boxes full of hoarded junk and other remnants of an era wearing out. This garage therefore, was also the secret meeting room for us, the children of the house.

The festival of *Holi* was nearing. The many trees in the largely unkempt grounds were shedding their yellowed leaves and the first splash of colours was being sprung by Mother Nature. On the day prior to the festival, my cousins, my brothers and I, were gathered in the garage, getting a fix on our inventory of colours. We were always short of money and prices were always going up, especially of the fast colours which were sold in small paper-folds. But this year we were equipped with knowledge – exciting, inflation beating, cottage-industry knowledge!! Today we were going to manufacture our own *"poteen"* – we were going to burn large quantities of paper and transfer the black residual powder into small bottles. This powder when mixed with mustard oil made a terrific black paste which would go nicely on all the faces we were determined to paint black on the morrow. There were many on our hit list – a specific older cousin, the neighbour's son, our miserly cook.....We had smuggled stacks of old newspapers and soon we had a fire going inside the large garage. We were almost done when our spy and informant, Samma (son of the cycle-repair *wala* across the road from our house) came running to tell us that we were being sought. That put an abrupt end to our industry and we quickly trooped out of the garage after hiding our powder filled bottles under a lumpy and rotting mattress.

An hour or two later, (it was late afternoon,) the family was startled out of the quietude by shouts from outside. This was followed by sounds of running and more shouting. We rushed out.

The garage was on fire. Till today none of us can recall exactly how events unfolded that eventful afternoon. We have disjointed images.....People rushing in and out of the house with buckets and containers.... water being thrown at the flames but falling well short.... my father standing motionless, stunned into temporary paralysis...... we, the guilty youngsters, standing safely away from him in a cowering huddle.....pandemonium all around and a great deal of cross-shouting.......orange flames and black smoke....... someone kicking at the padlocked door of the room adjoining the garage...... feeling the heat even at the safe distance we were standing at......

In all this jumbled and hazy recollection, a stranger stands out with shining clarity. I clearly remember him rushing up and handing his wrist watch to me (for safe keeping). I did not know him and I did not have the sense to ask him then who he was. He stands out because in no time at all he had stamped his reassuring authority over the scene. With quiet urgency, he explained the situation to the frontline helpers and set up a system for dealing with the fire. We would later recall with so much wonder at his simple intelligence – he got the rooms adjoining the garage emptied of all movable objects and redirected the water that was being collected and thrown so frantically yet ineffectually at the flames, to the walls and ceiling of the same rooms. He was a shining example of a captain leading from the front. Clearly, it was due to these moves that by the time the fire brigade arrived on the scene, apart from the garage that got gutted, no other serious damage was suffered. The fire did not spread.

At the first sound and sight of the red fire engine a loud cheer went up. The firemen in their indigo-blue uniforms quickly had massive jets of water cascading over the garage and outhouses. The flames were doused and the thick plumes of smoke reduced to dissipating wisps. The crisis was over.

Later that evening when the hullabaloo had died down, the family gathered together for the inevitable post mortem. Many theories were aired about the cause of the fire but thankfully nothing pointed its dreaded finger at us. We had never looked so innocent in our lives I am sure! And then when no one could come out with a plausible explanation, all of us started wondering about the stranger who had taken control of the situation till the fire brigade arrived. Who was he? Everyone looked at each other but once again no one had the faintest clue. Not even us. I then remembered and cried out, "He gave me his watch!" Everyone turned to me in surprise. "Yes," I cried, nodding my head vigorously, "the man in the blue checked shirt! He gave me his watch for safe-keeping." I searched the pockets of my shorts frantically but there was no watch to be found. The servants were summoned – they too clearly remembered the Good Samaritan but did not know who he was. We recalled that he had folded his trousers up to his knees to keep them dry. He had been wearing *hawaii chappals.* Someone recalled seeing him wheeling out of the gate on his cycle immediately after the fire engine had arrived.

In the final analysis, he had miraculously appeared on the scene, helped us avert a major disaster and once reassured that all was well, had quietly melted away. No one had even thanked him…….

All this happened half a century ago. Yet, when the remainder of my generation gets together every once in a few years, often times, like bicycles leaning against ancient walls, we pause and reminisce about those bygone days and that specific fire incident. We always wonder who that man in the blue checked shirt was, where had he come from and why had he just gone away? Always by instinct I also check my pockets for his watch and of course it's never there.

But it was on that fateful afternoon…..

The Unveiling

Placid waters heaved and churned,
Whirlpools on my head were found,
At her sight our heads were turned,
A younger brother almost drowned.
Those were mighty days I say,
Mrs. B could swing and sway!

I was and continue to be afraid of water. I often wonder - can I take a swim all alone at night in the pool downstairs? Through all the logic, sense and strength garnered over the years, the truth comes out unscathed – No, I can't….

This fear of water goes back to my infancy. One of my earliest memories is of my grandmother fretting over the fact that I had soft strands of hair curling in concentric circles over my temples. "These are symbols of a whirlpool" she would mutter while rubbing her fingers vigorously over the sides of my head. I would thus be regularly pinned flat across her outstretched legs and administered my first lessons in one-sided love. Not surprisingly, over a period of time, my dear old *Dadi* had literally rubbed the "whirlpools" away! But even as I bawled and howled, her "whirlpool" theory got indelibly registered inside my smarting head – the theory that those with *"bhanvars"* over their temples were destined to die by way of drowning. Even more than half a century later, that menace still lies in wait for me in the deep of dark and still water bodies.

I was born on the 4th of February. My Zodiac sign therefore is Aquarius. Quite ironical is it not that I carry the water-mark on me? Be that as it may, give me a bright swimming pool full of people splashing around and I will dive in gladly. I am a decent diver too!

As we grow older, we frequently keep going back to where our childhood lived. It's as if we need to keep retrieving treasures from there to help us through the present. Myriad images run through our mind. Some of these we hold to the light as it were and squint at them. We try to blow the dust away. We swipe at the years gone by like one would cobwebs while entering a long unused room. It has always made me wonder why certain images keep recurring over and over again. It is a mystery because it's not as if all such images represent milestones on the roads we once travelled.

One image that keeps recurring is of *Papa*, in white cotton trousers and bush-shirt, taking us in a *rickshaw* to the Bankipore Club for a swim. We used to be so many - five of us with our friends, my father with his friends and other members with their wards! It was a small pool and the water used to be changed once a week – on Sundays. *Papa* was such fun. We did not have a car those days – so on Sundays, he would take us to the Club in a *rickshaw-* not matter how hot it was. Patna's summer could be bad but my father's cheerful spirits easily prevailed over it. We used to be all over the seat and the footboard, clutching our towels wrapped around our swimming trunks. Just picture the mid-day scene - one adult and five children in one *rickshaw,* squeaking slowly over the dusty, largely quiet and soporific roads of a small town, chatting, jabbering, laughing and totally unmindful of the scorching sun beating down on us. Ridiculous or plain sweet – you decide.

During those days, in the forenoon of Sundays, Bankipore Club used to serve free potato chips with tomato sauce to visiting "dependents". Unbelievable (in today's context) but true. I have no recollection of when or why this practice got terminated but I suspect new members started using their wards as a front for getting free snacks for themselves. Or their wards themselves started to demand multiple helpings..........It never crossed our minds that rules could be broken. Those crisp and light, almost white potato chips, were out of this world. *Amma* and *Bari Amma* tried replicating that quality at home but in vain. They could not even get close.

Some of us liked to devour our share of chips (one plateful) immediately on reaching the club and some, like me, always kept the claim alive till after the swim. That particular Sunday, Papa was at the "deep" end with his friends, their beer mugs frothing and shining golden on the sides of the pool. We were splashing around in the shallow side. The more intrepid ones like *Bhaiya*, were running down the spring-board and diving into the deep end. There were some ladies in the pool too and we always experienced CTs (cheap thrills) watching them enter the pool from the corner of our eyes. There was one Mrs. Bhalla, whose entry used to be the only one of its kind. That day, she had sauntered into the pool area like a slow-moving ship, swaying and swinging, wrapped in her over-sized towel. The towel, we knew, would start getting peeled as the body started getting submerged in the water. The "unveiling" (or the absence of it) therefore started with the toes - the limb going in, the towel going out. It used to be such a tantalizing act. All activities ceased in and around the pool, I suspect even at the deep end where my father and his friends were! The climax of the act was the best of all. Mrs. Bhalla was now submerged to the waist, her splayed elbows touching the water and her plump fingers about to tear apart the overflowing and overstrained upper ends of her towel. And this she did with the speed of lightning. The towel flew out and Mrs. Bhalla fell in. The placid waters of the pool heaved and churned like a sea in turmoil as it tried its best to suck Mrs. Bhalla's modesty into its agitated depths. Just then there reached our ears, through all of Mrs. Bhalla's squealing and splashing, the plaintive cries of "help, glug, help"!

Startled, we looked around and saw to our horror, the horrified head of my younger brother (Yashi), going under. What was the guy doing in the deep side, my brain screamed. He didn't know how to swim! Yashi's head popped up again but this time only gurgling sounds came out of his gasping mouth. He went down again even as his flailing arms thrashed around helplessly......Simultaneously, in those frantic moments, several of us reached him and pulled him out safely. He looked stunned and disoriented as we sat him down on the side of the pool and ran our hands down his narrow tiny back. He must have been six or seven years old. We looked around scared but thankfully the elders at the other end had not noticed anything.

What had happened was that while our combined attention was focused on Mrs. Bhalla, young Mr. Y decided to take a leap into the deep side to emulate the feat of his eldest brother, who by now was an accomplished swimmer.

Sheel *Bhaiya* (my cousin) did something very sensible that day. He made Yashi jump into the water again from the spring board.

"Jump," he said to the scared youngster, "because if you don't jump now, you will never jump again."

He reasoned and cajoled. All of us saw the sense in what Sheel *Bhaiya* was trying to do. We assured

Yashi that we were there to take care of him and that nothing would happen this time. I even promised him that he could have my yet unclaimed plate of potato-chips… So the brave young Yashi jumped and of course *Bhaiya* and Sheel *Bhaiya* were there to hold him and ease him out…..He learnt how to swim soon after.

It struck my mind then that by some accident the whirlpool menace had missed its intended mark and that was why Yashi had been saved.

I shivered, as I frequently have, ever since.

CHINAMEN IN THE DARK

Black-out nights in sixty-two,
Chinamen hiding in the dark,
And, against this innocent fun,
At your command, the Home Guards:
My father, the head of all men,
Marching out of sync, the tall men...

During the time when the slow-wheeling fifties had given way to the romping sixties and Shammi Kapoor had burst on the silver screen with the original "YAHOO" signifying change of gear and colour like nothing before, I was on that cusp of life which is the most bewildering. I was still innocent and immature like boys in small towns used to be those days but I was also transitioning into manhood in awkward ways, not least by way of the cracks in my voice and uneven shadows on my face. The transition really becomes difficult because while the body undergoes changes almost by the day, the innocence of boyhood continues to ride along. The net result is the spectre of a loose-limbed gangly being that almost looks like a man but is ignorant like a boy. At least such was the case with me.

China invaded India in 1962. Not surprisingly therefore, it was an extremely exciting time for me even though it was a terribly wounding war for the country. We lost morale, face, territory and men. We lost so much and so emphatically, it wounded the psyche of the nation.

We had a cook those days by the name of Moti, who was as effeminate as he was informed. One day, when the war bulletin carried details of yet another major reversal, he threw up his hands in designer-despair and remarked, "If General Cariappa had been around, he would have won the war for us!"

I now realize - that singular observation by our cook provides such a telling profile of those times – we had leaders who were legends and we were a people who were proud of the nation.

I was not old enough to understand the implications of an invasion and neither was I enlightened enough to know that China was a much stronger and ruthless country, physically as well as politically. Conversely, I was in that phase of innocence when I knew no fear and understood no tragedy.

My first flight of fancy was to imagine Ram*cha* (my uncle - *Papa's* youngest brother) in his fighter plane engaging with the enemy in the sky and shooting them down. But the real situation was quite contrary. The IAF's fighters and bombers were totally invisible during the Indo-China War for the simple reason that they were not issued the orders to do so (out of fear of massive retaliation).

And so Ram*cha* (or any fighter pilot for that matter) did not take active part in that war. However, boys have the art of finding their way to happiness and action. My life soon got marked by multiple high points -

1) Spiraling air-raid sirens!
2) The consequent black-out drills when the entire city went dark and disembodied voices called out to each other!
3) Trips to the Indian Nation and Searchlight offices in the company of elders to read the latest news which used to be flashed on giant bulletin boards.
4) News of the war on the radio – *"ghamasaan yuddh"* is a phrase that still rings in my head.
5) The staples of wool the ladies of the house procured for the war effort – *Dadi* was a legendary knitter of sweaters and could put her daughters-in-law to shame with the speed and neatness with which she could knit. Between *Dadi, Bari Amma, Amma* and *Didi,* God knows how many sweaters were knitted for our *jawans* who were haplessly faced not only with a ruthless and rampaging enemy but also with the impending winter on the rocky heights of the Himalayan frontiers. I remember sitting in front of *Dadi,* holding the spools of multi-coloured wool across

and around my wrists while she spun them into balls before subjecting them to the magic of her knitting needles.

6) And last and also the most exciting of all – the Home Guards!

The Chief of Police (Mr. Duniya Lal I think) was a friend of *Papa's* and discussed with him the need to rustle up a band of volunteers (both men and women) who would get basic training in the use of fire-arms, first-aid and rescue work so that Patna would be ready with a local force to deal with emergencies in the event of it coming under attack. Mr. Lal was most skeptical about his ability to do so. My father assured him that he would be able to string together a force of such volunteers within a couple of days. This was a casual and off-the-cuff *tete-a-tete* between two friends but something quite momentous emerged out of it – the revival of The Patna Home Guards!

All it took my father was to ask a handful of close friends to come home for a war related discussion. He explained the issue to them and after that the social multiplier phenomenon took effect. *Amma* and *Bari Amma* too played their part because many *chachis, phuas* and *mausis* were wearing the regulation blue bordered white *sarees* and white socks and keds in no time at all. They looked funny and ungainly as they tried to fall in line at the parade ground but they made us so proud and for the first time ever in my life, I experienced the goose-bumps of patriotism. The men had khaki uniforms with leather shoes. It amazes me to think back and absorb the fact that those middle-class, peace-loving and insulated men and women from a relatively small town, were strutting about in uniforms in such a short time. They (*Amma* and *Didi* included,) had learnt how to use fire-arms, how to administer first-aid (including artificial respiration), how to tie a reef knot and bring down injured persons down bamboo ladders.....they were even taught the basics of the Morse-code!

(In later years I wore *Papa's* khaki shirts to College in Calcutta and started quite an unintended trend there!)

But back to the Home Guards!

My very own Arun*cha* (a very dear uncle who was living with us those days and trying to get a start in life through examinations and interviews) bagged the best shooter's award at the Bihta Firing Range where those magnificent men and women had been taken to give a display of their acquired skills and prowess. (30 kilometers out of Patna, Bihta was an army base of sorts).

But best of all was that *Papa* had been designated the Company Commander of the Home Guards! I recall with such clarity, the meetings that he used to hold at night in our large Drawing Room at our house on Exhibition Road - there were so many of them, the beat-captains, that the sofas had been shifted to one side and the uniformed men would sit around on the carpet with their regulation torches and discuss strategies and contingencies. Nothing can erase the image of the Home Guards participating in the march-past during the Republic day parade at the *Maidan* in January 1963 (the war having ended in the early winter of 1962) – *Papa* led his team in the parade from the front of course but the ladies were driven past the Governor and Chief Minister in open jeeps and lorries (not having mastered the art of marching in formation I guess). I must have clapped the hardest!

Arun*cha* (who was to become "partner" to me in subsequent years) was absolute fun. He and *Didi*, comrades in mischief, soon developed their private Morse-code and kept us in splits and exasperation with their remixed version of "da-did-did-da's" throughout those unforgettable years.

And the credit for perpetuating the first fraud on the Indian Telephone System also goes to the same Arun*cha* and this happened during the thick of the Chinese invasion in 1962. The Home Guards had to assemble early every morning at the Police Lines for drills and training. Now between Arun*cha* and Binnu *Chacha* (another uncle) who lived in *Kadam Kuan* (several kilometers away from Exhibition Road) there was just one alarm clock (at *Kadam Kuan*). The Company Commander (*Papa!!!*) had "instructed" Arun*cha* to wake him up every morning and this posed a problem because Arun*cha* did not have an

alarm clock. So he turned to his close friend Binnu
for help. Binnu *Chacha* said "no problem, I will wake
you up by giving you a phone call". But even local
calls cost money and since the waking up was being
done for the cause of the nation, why should the
woken-ups pay for it? So it was decided that Binnu
Chacha would give two rings and hang up. Hence no
cost would be incurred and both friends would wake
up. Arun*cha* was about to give a thumbs up to this
scheme but before he could do so, his razor-sharp
mind located another difficulty. What if the false
ring did not wake him up? Then what? He thought
and then he laughed. He would repeat what the first
caller had done. To confirm that indeed he had
woken up, Arun*cha* would give two false rings in
return. Binnu *Chacha* who was already up, would
know that his good friend was awake too!

The circuit thus completed, every morning, so
long as the Chinese created havoc on our Northern
Borders, Arun*cha* and Binnu *Chacha* continued to
rob the Indian Telephone system of two local calls
every morning!

Yes, those were the days my friend…. We knew
how to triumph, even in the dark!

THE FALSE BEARD

A Madrasi mystic, a sage from Madras,
A beard and a prank ending in a farce,
Kept out of bounds the soothsayer from Madras,
Surely he was lucky was not kicked in his arse.

When I realized for sure that girls were not taking much notice of me, I knew that the fault lay in my face. By then I had entered college at Calcutta.

My family background was top drawer, my college was top grade (almost), my height was good, my physique was better (slim), my complexion came with the *gehuan* "IS" *marka*…..yet, the fairer sex showed little or no interest in me. So finally deductive logic knocked on my bathroom door and I saw in the mirror what I had been merely looking at for so many years! I saw my face! I knew then that I had to hide or at least camouflage it. Thus was born my beard. And though spasmodically at the start, it has been bred and brought up, ever since.

Having thus established the origin of my beard, I can tell you for sure that the story that follows happened before I entered college. Because this story is about a false beard. I was a prankster and a joker in my teen years, especially in the secure environs of home and family. Hence, not surprisingly, like Enid Blyton's Fatty of the "Five Find Outers and Dog" series, I had, among other things, a false beard hidden somewhere in the famous garage that had once caught fire!

Our thinking always get misshaped with stereotypes. Those days, there were two which will surely find an echo in most of you. One stereotype was that all South Indians were "Madrasis" and the other was that all "Madrasis" kept saying "aiyyaioh", yum (for M), yen (for N) and so on...

As you may have guessed by now, the beard and the stereotype came together one unsuspecting afternoon. I wrapped a length of white cloth as a *lungi* or *mundu* around my waist, slipped a loose half sleeved shirt over my head (my father's I guess), created a head gear similar to that of Dr. S. Radhakrishnan, fixed the false beard in place with its wires that hurt, hid my tell-tale eyes behind dark glasses and....there must have been other appurtenances too which I cannot readily recall. I quickly rehearsed a few sentences and emerged from the garage, a Madrasi mystic.

In the quiet of that afternoon, I looked hither and thither and then walked resolutely up the front steps that led to the wide verandah of my home and knocked on one of the many doors.......

I will cut a long story short. I pulled off my act better than expected. So much so that my dear old *Dadi*, ever willing to listen to the words of the wise, even woke up her son, my father, from his week-end afternoon siesta to meet "the Sage from Madras". I lost my nerve then and hastily revealed my identity!

I must digress slightly here and tell you that my life, blessed as it is, has also been showered with uncles and aunts who have been great sports to share it with. One such was Panna Mama (the late Mr. M.S.Dayal). He had this great capacity of topping the popularity charts of both the young and the not so young! He was absolute fun and just the thought of him brings a smile to my face even today.

Well, the story of my well played out prank got tossed from one relative's mouth to another and finally fell into the lap of Panna Mama, ever on the lookout for fun and games. Panna Mama had a cousin from Kanpur (unknown and unmet but still a "mama" to me I suppose) who was visiting Patna to attend the wedding of his cousin's daughter. Now this "Kanpur Mama" was apparently involved in an ugly litigation with his brothers over a land dispute. His well-wishers (including Panna Mama) wanted the matter to get settled amongst the warring brothers amicably. But the question was - how could he get that noble end reached?.......Voila! His "eureka" moment suddenly jumped out of his lap!

I have no idea, no recollection whatsoever, of how Panna Mama convinced my elders at home that it was for a noble cause that he would take me to the Kanpur Mama (who incidentally was putting up at the house of the *shaadi-wale* Mama) in the garb of the SOOTHSAYER FROM MADRAS and get a potentially violent family dispute resolved with the tutored words distorted by a disguised teenager who could not even boast of having his own home-grown beard.

On the appointed evening therefore, Panna Mama came home, checked me up and down like a movie director-cum-costume-designer and drove me out of my tenterhooked home in his station wagon. On the way, he filled me with Kanpur Mama's family history and trivia, rehearsed responses to anticipated questions, added more Madrasi flavor to my yums and yens and laughed his throaty laugh. His cheerfulness was always infectious and I therefore knew that "all the world's a stage and all the men and women" and falsely bearded teenagers to boot, "merely players" who were there to play their noble parts….. So what was there to be nervous about?

To cut another long story short, I again pulled off my act with aplomb amongst a crowded audience which included a cornered Kanpur Mama who sat with bowed head and folded hands. He listened raptly to my wise yet edgy words and promised to end all acrimony and share the disputed land with his less fortunate brothers. Mission accomplished, we drove out of that happy house, straight to Panna

Mama's favorite haunt, "The Soda Fountain". He fed me with all that I wanted and as much as I wanted!

But as we all know, life is not just a comedy act. The secret got out the day before the wedding. The most outrageous and unforgivable part I suppose was that the lead actor in this farce was a mere and largely unconnected teenager. On the other hand, there was a wedding at hand. The spirit of the latter prevailed. Tempers cooled and good intentions were reluctantly understood and accepted.

But there still remained the danger that my beardless sight (which would show my true colors), might well trigger a distasteful reaction and ruffle smoothened feathers. So I was firmly advised to stay away.

I therefore missed a wedding, Panna Mama was (probably) censured like adults are by other adults during festive occasions and a false beard went permanently back into the annals of the richest garage that ever was which never had a car!

MR. X & RAMANATHAN KRISHNAN

When the good nuns strutted about,
Shepherding girls in navy skirts,
When the coffee without a doubt
Flowed poetic in metered spurts,
Then did the wonder years unfold
Legends and people rolled in gold.

When I last went to Patna, the city of my birth died on me even more than before. One had read reports about how the state of Bihar was showing resurgence under the leadership of its shiny new Chief Minister. Nothing shiny if one were to look at him and what I saw of the capital city therefore, only reflected this man's unwashed profile. Patna left me (or should I say, I left Patna) disgusted and deprived – it was filthy, it was squalid and it was chaotic.

But Patna used to be different during my "wonder years" – for one it had the best boys' school in the country and for another, it had the St. Joseph's

Convent where nuns strutted about in starch-stiffened habits and angels skipped around in White shirts and Navy Blue skirts. The Ganga flowed unsullied along its tree-lined length to the north. Tantalizingly peeping out of this green-peppered landscape, like a block of vanilla ice-cream, was the Bankipore Club where demure ladies swam and jaunty men swilled beer. There was the famous coffee house where writers like "Renu" and "Dinkar" sat surrounded by students measuring poetry by the metre and coffee by the yard. And whenever you passed by the Martyrs' Memorial, you bowed to the Nation's flag held aloft by sculpted men and women in the throes of revolution and death.

There was this, there was that, and finally there was on Exhibition Road, this square-shaped house with a huge compound where boys grew up in a family which taught them right from wrong...........
Patna was a slow wheeling, content and happy town those days with clean residential localities, teeming bazaars, serpentine lanes, open drains, caring people, street-friends and fresh green grass.

Fresh green grass!!

Apart from the iconic Bankipore Club, there was the New Patna Club too – a poor cousin of the first but with an appendage that few clubs in the country could boast of. It once hosted the International Davis Cup tournament (that too, India versus Pakistan) on its smooth-as-velvet grass courts. The handsome Haroon Rahim was given a lesson in court-craft by the wily Jaideep Mukerjea in the decider and I was one of the linesmen.

Patna was a thriving tennis centre those days. It had an annual feature called the Bihar Lawn Tennis Championship (BLTC) which all the National players of rank and repute attended. For those familiar with that era and that sport, the following names will evoke some memory and some wonder – S.P Mishra, Gaurav Mishra, Sashi Menon, Shyam Minotra, C.G.K.Bhupathi (father of Mahesh Bhupathi), Anand Amrithraj, Vijay Amrithraj, Premjit Lall, Jaipdeep Mukerjea and, hold your breath…..Ramanathan Krishnan! There used to be a host of other upcoming players too. They came from all parts of the country. And believe it or not, sometimes local wannabes like me even got a chance to play against these great players in the first round. Some also got to "umpire" the initial rounds….. Those truly were the days my friend!

Krishnan has been the best tennis player by far that India has ever produced. Some of you will know, but some may not - he reached the Wimbledon Singles Semi Finals twice and in both years lost to the eventual Champion (Neale Fraser and Rod Laver respectively). He was once ranked 4th in the world. No Indian has come anywhere close to this level of International achievement in this sport.

Krishnan was also an absolute gentleman. And he was modest to a fault. He had two endearing habits which will bear testimony to what I am saying. (1) If his opponent was given a bad call by a linesman, Krishnan would invariably lose the next point. And (2) when he played against players who should not have wasted his time, he would never beat them 6-0, 6-0. It would invariably be 6-0, 6-1 or 6-1, 6-0.

There was this unforgettable incident that took place one year. It was the first round. I was the umpire sitting on a high stool in charge of Court Number 1 (there used to be six grass courts) and Krishnan was playing one of "us" – I forget his name, so I will call him X.

X lost the toss but Krishnan asked him to serve. X served. X "won" the game. Please pause and digest this. By winning the first game of the first set, X was actually leading against India's top seed! So you should forgive X if his head got muddled with "headlines" during that fraction of his life. This muddling must have happened, otherwise you just cannot explain X's behavior that followed...

As per rules, the two players crossed sides - Krishnan bored yet pleasant but X, demonic and muttering. I strained my ears and heard "Attaboy boy. Concentrate. You can do this...." Aghast, I looked at X but he was looking at the "headlines". Krishnan took the next game. 1-1. X served – with all his might. He lost: Krishnan leading 2-1. They again crossed over. This time X looked at me and shook his head. Umpires are supposed to maintain decorum. So I looked away hastily. Krishnan held his serve (naturally) and led 3-1. Now it was again X's turn to serve. He tossed the ball in the air a few times and it looked as though he was checking which way the wind was blowing! Did he really not know? Krishnan slouched at his base line patiently. X again unleashed all his might and served.

"FAULT," I called.

X looked at me incredulously. "What?" he asked. "Fault" I repeated. "But the linesman, why is there no linesman?" he demanded, as if he didn't know. Krishnan looked at me uncomprehendingly. So I explained to him that X thought the serve was in. "Oh ah." He smiled, winked and nodded. There was in his countenance a plea which said please get on with the game. So I awarded the point to X. But X lost the next 4 points because bafflingly, each return of serve from Krishnan landed at spots where even X's shadow did not reach.

4-1 Krishnan leading now and the two of them crossing over – Krishnan cool but X hot like Casablanca on his *burning deck whence all but he had fled*. I took pity.

"*Kya hua*?" I asked.

X looked at me as one would from a sinking ship. "*Kya bolen yar, aaj mera service jaiyye nahi raha hai!*"

No LOL those days or ROFL either. But that day an umpire lost his decorum and I FOTHSL (Fell Off The High Stool Laughing)!!

PAUPERS TO KINGS

There came a time when we took wing,
When boys turned into men,
When paupers could turn into kings
As fast as now and then!

That summer holiday in Senior School, I informed my family that I would not be accompanying them to Darjeeling. Instead, I would be staying back to prepare for the National Defense Academy (NDA) exams because I wanted to become an Air Force Pilot. Everyone was stunned because till then I had never given any evidence that I could be focused and decisive.

I stayed behind. I studied, I toiled and I took the written exams. Not surprisingly one day a letter arrived to say that I should present myself at Varanasi to face the grueling SSB (Services Selection Board).

Some days later, my black steel trunk, khaki hold-all and I were at the Varanasi railway station. The platform on which I stood was swarming with other young men with hold-alls and steel trunks.

"I am Dhillon. I am from the Dalli ya!" A tall young Sardar was smiling at me and shaking my hands. He had the most likeable face one could have hoped for in the circumstances. This one gesture right at the start of my tryst at the Varanasi Station, exemplified the bonhomie that we youngsters enjoyed during those fateful four days at the Army cantonment.

I cleared the SSB along with the dreaded PABT (Pilot Aptitude & Battery Test) that all air-force aspirants had to clear. I was then asked to proceed to Delhi from Varanasi itself to face the last hurdle – the CME (Central Medical Examination).

My elder brother was in college at Delhi those days. I shacked up with him. We would be traveling together to Patna because his holidays had begun.

Everything seemed to go well during the CME except that during the vision test I was squinting, squirming and guessing. Finally, the tired looking Squadron Leader told me the bitter truth. When, in utter desperation I asked him, "But sir, doesn't short-sightedness improve with age?" he just patted me and walked away.

When I met up with my brother, he was insanely cool. Nimbly side-stepping my crashed dreams he announced that he would take me to 'The Cellar' at CP. He was a "Stephenian" and he knew what that meant to a younger sibling who was still in school in Patna! "Give me your wallet" he said. I gave it to him. He looked inside it and then he looked at me.

"Where's the money?" he asked.

"What money?" I asked.

"*Arre* your money," he said.

"That's all I have" I said.

He stared at me in disbelief. He kept staring......
Anyway the long and the short of it was that we were
both broke. Between us we had just about enough
to pay for our train tickets to Patna.

But youth is all about taking long strides. And
therefore, sitting across each other in the crowded
coach of the Upper India Express, The Cellar was
forgotten and my shattered dream was side-lined.
We were just two happy young brothers going home!
Life was as simple as that.

I think the train took in excess of 12 hours from
Delhi to Patna those days. *Bhaiya* who was now in
charge, took stock and concluded that we could
afford just one meal during the journey - at Mughal
Sarai. But even after a couple of hours, Mughal Sarai
was hours away and one hour was made of 60
minutes and 1 minute was 1 hour long.......

After what seemed like a life time, the train
steamed into Mughal Sarai station. We staggered out
and feasted on *poorie-tarkari* which the vendor gave
us in *donas* made from dry leaves. We ate and we ate
and once again home was just a few more hours
away. After all what were six or seven hours in the
context of a life time?

We reached Patna Junction at around nine in
the night. *Bhaiya* hailed a coolie and when I looked

at him in alarm, his eyes commanded me to shut up. On reaching the stands outside, he first hired the rickshaw that would take us home. He then helped the coolie unload the luggage directly on its foot board. Having booked and cooked both of them, he then asked the incredulous rickshaw-*wala* to pay off the coolie. *Bhaiya* was cool and he was collected. A smallish crowd started to collect around us because the coolie and the rickshaw-*wala* were not cool and collected.

"I will pay back the money and the fare after we reach home," my brother explained. He showed our empty wallets and pockets to the whole crowded world which was watching the scene by now. I pulled up the hood of the rickshaw to hide my cringing self.

"Where do you have to go?"

"Exhibition Road."

"Where on Exhibition Road?" the man insisted. My brother explained where exactly. He was even trying to describe the house when the rickshaw puller asked in disbelief.

"*Daagdar Babu ke ghar jana hai aap log ko*?" Yes, yes we exclaimed in unison. We hailed from a joint family and our father's elder brother, *Babuji*, had been a well known doctor.

"*Hey Bhagwan*, you boys belong to *that* family? And you do not have money to pay a *coolie*?" He gave us a withering look and muttered something under his breath which my brother did not like. But it was that time, in that kind of night, when you can only swallow – air, pride, fear, saliva, whatever.

As he pedaled through the relatively dark night, the rickshaw-*wala* kept looking back at us with both distaste and suspicion. Were we for real? He kept cross-examining us repeatedly about the address we had given. When *Bhaiya* expressed outrage at the man's persistent questioning, the fellow asked, "*Aap hi bataiye Babu, koi bade ghar ka aadmi ricksha-wala se paisa mangta hai?*"

He made us feel small with his verbal assaults, but in our hearts we knew he was justified. When I look back, I say to myself "poor man". But the fact is that during that ride back home we were the real paupers.

Finally we were on Exhibition Road. Our beloved home, which stood square and luminous in back of the large grounds that fronted it, came into view. The portico was lit and our green Studebaker parked smartly under it. We turned off the road.

But in that instant, it was not just the rickshaw that had turned - the two brothers sitting in it had also turned – from paupers into kings once again.

JEETENDRA & GOVINDA

A moment was lost,
A perspective gained,
Nice guys, both of them
By stardom were claimed.

As a youngster I was obsessed with films. Bombay was a dream and distant destination and movie stars were celestial bodies. I had my favourites but there were also some I did not think much about.

One "star" I absolutely looked down upon, was Jeetendra. I hated his white pointed shoes, his crude dance moves, his diction, his voice and his absolutely unremarkable face! Yet, the irony of fate, he happened to be the first of the few leading actors from Bollywood I have had the occasion to encounter.

I was in senior school and Jeetendra had come to Patna during the shooting of his movie "Dharti Kahe Pukar Ke". The slow-wheeling city of my birth was shaken out of its daily monotony. So also was dislodged someone's hoity-toity attitude! With the cart-wheeling ability one has as a youngster, I spat my disdain out of the window, lowered my skyward nose and met up with my pals to plot a plan to meet the "Hero from Bombay" who was put up at the only decent hotel those days – Hotel Republic. This hotel was literally a stone's throw from my home on Exhibition Road. Jeetendra was a star and we knew that it would not be easy to get access to him.

Who had heard of customer-profiling, marketing and branding those days. But by instinct we knew that our anglicized school (St. Xavier's) was our "Unique Selling Proposition". So we drafted a letter to Jeetendra in the Queen's English, appealed to his good judgment and sought an audience with him. We signed the letter as "Four Jesuit Students". Since Hotel Republic was on "my" road, I led the 4-strong delegation through the throng of unruly fans crowding the barricaded entrance of the hotel and managed to thrust the letter through the collapsible gate into the hands of one of the hotel staff, saying that the letter should be delivered to the star immediately. To our unexpected delight, the strategy worked. Somewhere in America a young Peter Drucker was pollinated!

A few minutes later, the four of us were standing in a carpeted corridor and knocking on a polished door. It opened and there was Jeetendra - in a *lungi-kurta*, smiling down at us and welcoming us into his suite. Another man, similarly clad, was in the room. He too shook our hands. We soon realized the other man was the "sidey" villain, Manmohan. With a cigarette between his lips and drink in hand, he looked sleazy in real life too.

Jeetendra put us at ease by his friendly manner. He sipped slowly from his glass and spoke very little about himself. On the contrary, he made us tell him about ourselves – family, school, studies... In no time at all we were absolutely at ease – Jeetendra even made us feel good about ourselves because he confessed that he had not had the privilege of good education and hence envied us. Presently, he went into an adjoining room and returned with a box of sweets.

"Please have some" he said to us. "They are delicious. I believe they are called *khaja*!"

I think Manmohan was feeling left out. Perhaps he was also misled by Jeetendra's unhurried hospitality and our easy English - because suddenly, out of the blue, he was offering us cigarettes and drinks. One from us, Mukul I think, even reached out to accept a cigarette.

Jeetendra stepped in then. He chided his fellow actor in a quiet even voice. He reminded him that we were school boys from very respectable backgrounds. "Instead of offering them Coca Cola, you are offering them alcohol and cigarettes?"

That put an end to any further adventurism and soon after we took our leave. Jeetendra came up to the door and shook our hands. He looked at us wistfully and said "It was a privilege meeting you four!"

We came out feeling tops. Jeetendra had made us feel good about ourselves. But the true measure of his graciousness was understood by us in later years. At the time, we were too taken up by his stardom and our sense of self-achievement at having had a private *tete-a-tete* with him. Today I feel very good about him. In my eyes, his graceful ageing provides evidence of his innate decency. Or am I just being sentimental? I leave it you to decide that.

* * *

I encountered Govinda many years later. He too was a super-star when I came across him and he too was someone whose movies I refused to watch, even on TV. Need I go into the reasons for my dislike? "Sarkai de khatiya…." would suffice I suppose.

I was on a flight to Hyderabad from Bombay with my father and so also was Govinda. He had created enough commotion on the flight by just being there. Passengers kept crowding around him to shake his hands and talk to him. Govinda stood in the aisle and flashed his toothy smile and generally basked in the adoration surrounding him. I explained to my father who he was.

We finally landed. I do not remember how this happened but while descending the steps, my father got sandwiched between Johnny Lever (who was also on the flight) and Govinda himself. I was directly behind Govinda. While Johnny Lever traipsed down with aplomb, my father, very frail of body, had to hold the railing and descend one step at a time. In so doing he was holding up the super star right behind him. I was amazed to observe then that not only did Govinda not make a fuss or try and bypass by father, but all along the slow descent, he was totally focused on my father lest he slipped or lost a footing. Govinda was vigilant behind him just as I, the son, would have been. When both of them were on the tarmac, he turned around to see if anyone was with my father. I nodded my head to him. I wanted to reach out to him and thank him but I guess I was too shy. The moment was lost because in the next instant he was already moving away and getting claimed by the stardom that was his.

I caught up with my father and pointing in the direction of the swiftly fading star said, "Nice guy!" My father looked at me quizzically and said, "Oh, but I thought you did not like him!"

POPE'S PORTRAIT

Sometimes,
When it is time to prove our worth,
The time to turn and say our grace,
We throw our pens and raise the sword,
With hollow might we end our race.
We hoist a flag in the dark,
And hark, hark, the dogs do bark.

My educational background is something I am very proud of. I thank my stars for the same because this is one area where I can't, even in my most self-pitying moments, deny that I got lucky!

It all started with St. Xavier's High School at Patna; then (after getting rejected by St. Stephen's College, where both my brothers studied), I still had time to travel by train (unreserved) from Delhi to Calcutta and literally walk into St. Xavier's College; and finally, (because I did not want to join Avery India Ltd. as a Sales Representative at Siliguri) I got pushed into XLRI and became an "MBA"!

In terms of name and fame, XLRI ranks a clear first followed by St. Xavier's College, Calcutta. My beloved school is clearly at the bottom of the list. But (ironically) it's my school that I am the most proud of – and my profile page on Face Book is proof!

I have relatives and friends who went to Doon School, Mayo College, Netarhaat, Lawrence School, St. Columba's......I am happy they went there, no question – it's just that they did not go to the best school there ever was.

So Sonam, Amitabh, Blondie, Sundar, Koppa (to name just five), before you shake your heads, please match the following list of sports and extra-curricular activities that my school exposed its students to (apart from excellent academics) - Football, Cricket, Hockey, Volleyball, Basketball, Baseball, Handball, Tennis, Table Tennis, Swimming, Shuffle-Board, Singing, Wood Craft, Debates, Elocution, Extempore Speaking, Dramatics, Photography, Cinema and "Literary" societies...

And lest I forget - Athletics! Other than sprints and long distance running, we were exposed to Javelin Throw, Shot Putt, Long Jump, High Jump, Triple Jump.... However, since we were not perfect, we did not have Pole Vault I have to admit. So we still had greater heights to climb before a well meaning but ill-advised simpleton by the name of Karpoori Thakur came on the scene as Bihar's Chief Minister....But that's forgettable history now, so let me take you back to my school....

By the time I had established myself in Senior School, I was afflicted by a strange yearning – to prove myself. You see, all these years I had been a cat at home but a mouse in school. From the guava tree and with Samma alongside on the adjoining branch, I was king of all I surveyed, especially with my slingshot (*gulel*) in hand. But within the precincts of St. Xavier's, I used to be as grey and shrunk as the creature I had sent my bright green missiles slamming towards. Our school Principal, Fr. Gordon Edward Murphy, had once exasperatedly put a comment under my bewildered mug-shot in the Xavier Year Book – "Rajvardhan had brothers with reputation but....."

So the "also ran" had to find a race which he could win. It became a thing with me as shadows started to creep over my face. I became a rebel without a cause looking for a cause, meaning I became a rebel without a pause if you can get what I mean. I was not a man but I wanted to prove that I was. The straggly beard and moth-eaten moustache that accompanied me to senior school added to the pressure on me. Oh I was such a poor young sod. Mine was a sorry state of affairs, so if you are unfortunate enough to ever come across shady B&W photos of me in those days, forgive me!

St. Xavier's, as the name suggests, was run by Christian missionaries. Not surprisingly, most of the menial staff had been "induced" into the "faith". So we had a surfeit of Georges and Williams and Johns sweeping the corridors, cleaning the grounds, cooking food for the "boarders", serving them cocoa and keeping us safe and guarded….In Senior School you became "aware" of these subtle deviations from the norm even though (and I must state this) the inducements were soft and quiet and totally unobtrusive.

But there was one Langat Singh. Dark, robust, hard working and cheerful, he stood out because he was forever visible, his bare-back glistening under the sun while he laboured with odd jobs in the large grounds that housed our imposing school building. And he stood out also because of his name – not because of how it sounded but because of what it implied. For the likes of me, desperately looking for a "cause", he came as a ready-made and shiny rallying point of (hushed) rebellion against the "establishment". More imagined than researched that he was given the toughest and most menial jobs because he had shunned "conversion", we *heed & hawed* about the unfairness of it all. It felt good to be stung by something I could finally point my finger at. Poor Langat Singh, ever cheerful and uncomplaining, knew not that he had become the catalyst for some long dark faces in long white pants….

Please let me clarify lest you get misled by my narrative - there was no simmering "rebellion" building up in Senior School under the largely imagined *"atyachaar"* that Langat Singh was being subjected to. Not even by the longest shot that the School football captain could kick! My chums and I were merrily going about the business of growing up in some very high quality atmosphere and under some extremely high quality exposure. Yes, like some young men do, some of us did give dark looks to the white skinned padres who ironically (most of them at least) were going about their business of converting rough-cut boys into finely honed men! Therefore, effete rebels like me were having their cake and eating it too.

It took a couple of years before dark looks took the shape of dark designs and the portrait (oil painting of Pope Paul VI) which smiled down beatifically at any one who entered the school's "corridor of fame" from the eastern side, became the object of much destructive planning...

It was a cold winter night. It was Sunday and the school hall was packed to the rafters. The weekly Hollywood movie was on. My memory is pretty sharp but I can't for the world of me recall which movie it was – I am stating this to give you a measure of my tensed state of mind. I was about to step into the night you see.

We were two of us. We stepped out of the hall unnoticed. Our mufflers and dark jackets (all meticulously pre-planned of course), helped us slip like shadows in the night. We made our way into the dark corridor, lifted the portrait off the wall, slipped it under my loose long-coat and walked rapidly away towards the school gate. Our biggest worry was Remy, the school *darwan*. Now that there was no turning back, my heart thumped like it has only once since. The feeble portico light of the school never shone so brightly but luckily Remy was not perched on his stool.

The next steps were a mad frenzy. If you were to step out of the St. X gate at night those days, you would have a circular road curling silently in front and away. But immediately beyond this "C" of the road you would not see much. An expanse of utter darkness would beckon you, especially if you were of the mind of two utterly misguided co-conspirators. It was the perfect setting for a crime scene and I wish I could tell you that "Chase A Crooked Shadow" was the movie we had just walked out of…

My friend had brought some tools with him and with the help of these and our sturdy limbs, we destroyed the Pope's portrait in the pitch-dark *Maidan* that night – what had been one single piece of art now lay splintered into several insane parts. Oh how we flexed our muscles with the bravado of cowards. We did not stop there. After collecting each broken piece with meticulous care, we whistled and walked. Our destination: St. Joseph's Convent (the all-girls' counterpart of our school). The Convent, for obvious reasons, had high boundary walls. We flung the Pope (or what was left of him) over these walls. Then we went our ways. It was a bitterly cold and deserted night. Dogs howled in the distance and the occasional car scurried past like bright eyed rats.

What lay shattered behind us was not the Pope's Portrait but innocence, but we were too innocent to comprehend this then. Or were we?

St. Stephen's Ahoy

St. Stephen's beckoned so we boarded a train,
College we reckoned was a dance in the rain,
Freshers and ragging,
Nerds who kept bragging,
And "immortal" became the "Teep-Taap" refrain.

If (ironically), my objective of wanting to get into the Indian Air Force (when I was in Senior School) had shown a precocious clarity of vision, then what followed immediately thereafter was an equally unmitigated show of utter directionlessness. Take for example the six subjects I chose for my Senior Cambridge exams: English Language, English Literature, Hindi (B), Chemistry, History and Biology! To top it all, I failed in Bio! And I ended up with 24 points!

For those who are not familiar with the Senior Cambridge points system of that era, 24 points spelt a very mediocre 2nd Division. The best possible was "5 points" meaning getting an "A1" (90% and above) in your top five subjects. Yashi managed this rare distinction 4 years later which apart from making us insanely proud, also drove home the maddening fact that I had indeed been sandwiched between brothers with a reputation!

We assess ourselves very differently from our parents – at least such was the case with me. So while all the elders at home (especially my father), celebrated my Senior Cambridge results, I sulked and moped because I had not passed in the 1st Division. It hurt to see that no one else thought like I did.

Bhaiya was studying at St. Stephen's College at Delhi and so after the long 6 month vacation (following the Senior Cambridge exam), it was to Delhi that I headed along with many of my class-mates. St. Stephen's was the most coveted college in the country those days (especially for students in pursuit of a University degree in Humanities/ Arts). With a severe Second Division in tow, I had little chance of getting in but when you are young you die hard!

I can still feel the romance of that place. The Delhi University area was teeming with aspirants like me and there was a sense of bonhomie in the air which was very different from what we had ever experienced before. The girls were beautiful and electric and the boys cool. We were branded as "freshers" and it gave us a heady sense of both fear and belonging just to be summoned by that name by a group of senior students lounging in the

shade with cigarettes dangling from their disdainful
lips.

We were "ragged" and it was all quite fun in the
ultimate analysis. We were made to do such harmless
stuff like describing our sisters' physical features or
pushing a coin from one end of the verandah to the
other with our noses.....all this and similar stuff
even before we were given admission. The trick was
to behave respectfully and docilely – in the end, the
(so called) tormentors would sometimes even put
an arm around our shoulders and offer us a lick
from their sticks of ice-cream! But there were two in
my group who were not so lucky and you can see
why.

One was a tall bespectacled school-topper from
Calcutta whom we had befriended in the train which
had brought us to Delhi. When he was asked to give
his name, he had looked at the sky and said, "I think
I have forgotten it!" No sooner had shiny-specs
responded so than we heard the collective slurp of
hungry tongues followed by the chorus, "Oh really!
Come, come with us you amnesiac, we have been
waiting for you!" They took him with them while we
slunk towards one of the quiet staircases inside the
college building. An hour or two later our teary eyed
nerd, looking humbled and chastened, found us
and announced loudly that he was a "motherfucker".
"What?" we chorused. Quickly, he looked over his
shoulders and whispered that he was following
orders. All of us immediately started babbling in

whispers. When we finally went quiet, our man informed us with the wisdom of a ghost returning from the gallows that no matter what happened in future, we should not do push-ups when ordered to do so. "Why" we chorused once again. Because then, said shiny-specs, they would have made you prove to yourself that you were a "motherfucker". And they will then also make you walk up to every girl or boy in sight and inform them loudly that you were a "motherfucker". When he saw our uncomprehending faces, he smiled a bitter smile and said, "You losers, you don't get it do you?" We looked at him blankly and waited. "Push-ups, you idiots; on the floor; on **Mother**-earth!" he hissed and gestured lewdly with his hands. "Got the picture? Got it now? Don't do push-ups *yar*." So saying he put his head down, started shaking it and wailed softly, "*Maa, maago, khoma korro maaa...*"

The second was our very own school-mate Amarnath Jaiswal (of *teep-taap**fame). Amar had started to feel so much at home in the laid back surroundings of Delhi University that after answering a lone-wolf what his name was, he tried to get into the wolf's pack by asking in return, "And what is yours?" There followed a silence of the snapping-sound type. The guy stared at Amar in disbelief for some time. He then shook himself before informing all of us that his name was "SIR".

"Sir, till further notice" he added curtly. Then tapping Amar on the chest he added, "And Fresher, tomorrow morning at 9 sharp, you will walk up to me and say "Good Morning Sir. Got it?".

"Yes Sir", Amar stuttered.

The loner then turned to us. "Fuck off," he barked. We hurriedly did.

As far as our collective intelligence went and the nerd's, that was the end of the matter and Amar had been extremely lucky to be let off with just a moderate reprimand. But Amar was a shattered man. His misplaced confidence of moments ago had been replaced by limb-twitching paranoia. Next morning as the needles on his wrist watch moved inexorably towards the 9 a.m. deadline, Amar became more and more frantic in his search. He did finally spot "Sir" who was hanging out with a group of friends and immediately broke away from us before we could stop him.

"Good morning Sir" he piped out shrilly and bowed deeply.

Heads turned, eye-brows shot up, eyes narrowed….. And then there was silence. Pulsating silence. Frozen, we watched in horror. Something had to give. And it finally did - the dreaded slurping sound rose from the group like a howl from the wild, a collective drawing in of drool by a pack of hungry hunters on being suddenly served with the rare and blood-streaked dish called "prey-on-a-platter"…..

Amar was returned to us in a strangely flushed condition. He had thick curly hair when he was taken away but when he staggered back his hair was lank and wet and he had the washed out look of a dog unpacked. He had been given a head bath you see, a "flush-bath!"

Teep-Taap Amar:

\- We used to have an annual "Spring Fair" in school – a social event full of fun with game stalls, food-stalls and music. This was the only occasion when girls from the St. Joseph's Convent were officially brought to our school in buses. A few legendary romances blossomed during this event but by and large the rest of us simply picked out individual girls and declared them as 'mine' and remained totally contented with such one-sided arrangements till time and tide did do us apart!

The Spring Fair naturally attracted many townsfolk and some lumpen elements too. In our Senior Cambridge year, an unsavory incident took place – a boy (an outsider obviously) groped one of the Convent girls. There was commotion but several of us reached the spot in no time. We settled matters with ruthlessness in a dark corner and then with matching gentleness, for news had spread and we were now turning heads rapidly, guided the disoriented lout out of the premises. Our school Principal, Fr. Murphy, also got to know that an incident had occurred and came rushing to us to inquire. Amar was at hand and explained that it had been nothing - one boy had simply misbehaved with a girl but it had been clarified to him that such behavior was unacceptable and furthermore, after having been provided with such clarification, he had been escorted out of the school's premises. "What boy, what did he do?" Fr. Murphy persisted. Amar was twitching for such a chance anyway. So he immediately made graphic use of his hands and demonstrated to the school Principal what exactly had happened while elaborating that such cheap acts by chaps were normally referred to in colloquial Hindi as *Teep-Taap*!!!!

Amar did not realize that in that shocking, one-off instant he had literally made himself "amar" (immortal) because never had a St. Xavier's student ever uttered such tripe, that too supported by such artless handicraft in front of a teacher, much less the Principal, and never had the very composed and formidable Fr. Gordon Edward Murphy withdrawn from any scene more quickly and more redly!

JAMES BOND

'tween the dawn and the shimmering noon,
between the footfalls and the gloaming,
boys will be boys in questing the moon,
walls with slogans and naxals roaming....

This happened way back in the shimmering past, one summer afternoon in Gariahat at Calcutta. My Part I University exams were imminent and I had stepped out of my uncle's (Girish *Chacha*'s) flat to buy a bottle of ink.......

The eponymous Naxalbari had just stamped its presence on the Indian map in the colour of blood because it was from here that Charu Mazumdar & Kanu Sanyal had shot the first arrow of armed struggle to redistribute land to the landless. These two not only led committed Maoist cadres towards violence and terrorism in the country-sides but even caught the imagination of university students across large swathes of the country. "Naxalite" became a badge that many youngsters aspired to own – among these were genuine intellectuals, equally unblemished pseudo-intellectuals and unemployed street -loose vagabonds looking for a shiny cloak to wear. By the time I entered college, even the capital city – Calcutta - was teeming with "naxalites", both genuine and pseudo. The genuine ones were holding clandestine meetings, distributing seditious literature, writing revolutionary slogans on walls and lobbing bombs and killing policemen at random. The pretenders, in unbuttoned boat-collared shirts and drain-pipe trousers, were carving out *"padas"* (territories) for themselves to indulge in varying degrees and types of hooliganism.................

Yet, for the likes of me, life trundled along and one hopped on to a tram and moved through the city of strife at a strangely even and unhurried pace....

That afternoon the heat seemed to have bleached the outdoors and numbed it into a state of utter sloth. Nothing stirred. The tops of buildings and trees shimmered like card-board cut-outs against the dazzling sky. The heat hung limply in white-hot sheets in front of me and as I willed myself to maneuver through it, I was constantly wrapped in its clinging embrace.

Those days I was a student of St. Xavier's College and living under the roof and care of Girish Chacha and Sunila Chachi. My address: "P-15, Gariahat Lane" next to the unforgettable "P-16". My days were largely uneventful and my nights mostly filled with moons and stars which occasionally sparkled and shone. The block where I lived was quiet and largely residential and that day I had run out of ink. I had just reached the main Gariahat Road in the dead of that afternoon when I heard the taunt "Hey James Bond" which was followed by some sniggering. I stopped and peered into a shaded doorway – three youngsters - two boys and a girl - were looking at me with faces bearing tell-tale remnants of a smirk. I should have moved on but I did not. I was nervous, I was anxious, I was on edge. The slogan on the wall screamed at me to smash the mouths that fed on me..... The venomous serpent that pulses in the dark confines of most young men but stays largely inert, uncoiled. It was just one such slithering afternoon in Calcutta.

I stopped and turned. There was surprise and consternation amongst the three who watched me approaching them. There was confused movement. I recognized the brother and sister but the third was a new quantity. It was to him I went. I caught his collar, called him a bloody bastard. I hissed and spat and pushed him with all my strength. Even as he fell back, the brother-sister duo disappeared inside their door, shutting it behind them with a rattle. I glared at my cowering adversary for some moments. Then I swung around and started to walk away. Moments later he came from behind and landed a terrible blow on me. I staggered and spun and then I caught him in a vicious head-lock which I knew he could never get out of. He started to grow limp after thrashing about for a few moments. Someone separated us. I was taken aback by the number of people that had accumulated. My adversary came into his own then and started to speak rapidly to the onlookers. I knew enough Bengali to comprehend what he was saying:

I was an outsider. I had been misbehaving with a girl and harassing her. The reputation and dignity of the locality (*pada*) was at stake. And when he had rightfully confronted me about this, I had attacked him….blah blah and more blah.

So it was all about the girl I realized with utter disdain and disgust. I defended myself as best I could but I could not speak *Bangla* those days. The mixture of Hindi and English set me up as an outsider and I could sense this. But the neighborhood was good, those people were reasonable, my face was honest….We were told to go our separate ways. There was disbelief on the face of the vanquished as he raced away shouting, "You wait hee-yar, you wait hee-yar. I will come back." One well meaning guy patted my back and advised me to go underground. I bought ink and walked back home apprehensively. As I turned into my lane, I could see not a soul. The scenario was as stark and soul-less as before. The doors were shut. The shadows were asleep….. Once I was safely inside my home, my knees went limp and I vomited.

In the days that followed I did see that fellow in the distance on a few occasions but nothing happened. My exams began and luckily the center allotted to me was a college near Gol Park which was a stone's throw from home. There was a posse of policemen at the gate. They looked edgy. Bombs, knives and brawls were not unknown in exam centers those days.

We were hardly twenty minutes into our paper when we heard a commotion outside - sounds of shouting and running feet. Next moment the door of our first floor exam hall burst open and a bunch of hoodlums rushed in, raising slogans and throwing things around. We were ordered to tear up our papers and walk out. We froze. Our brave invigilator stood his ground. Where was the police, I wondered. The very next moment I was staring into the face of a bad dream. He was standing just a few feet from me and he was staring back. The commotion around me got distanced by the pounding in my head. I held his gaze even as the sweat from my face ran icily down my neck. Just then a bedraggled young man came running and shouted something from the door. The goons in our hall rushed out. Before turning away, my friend, my foe, nodded his head at me. Then he too rushed out and ran down the stairs. It took us a few minutes to realize that the storm had blown over….We broke into animated cross talk but when the invigilator clapped sharply, we went back to sanity. In no time at all the only sounds that could be heard was the drone of fans and of nibs scratching over paper. I took a bit longer than the others to get my blood and ink back into circulation.

It's strange but I never saw that guy again. So many years have gone by but I still cannot figure out why he left me alone, especially that day in the exam centre. He had the upper hand and he was the wronged party. He had merely called me James Bond whereas I had abused him by calling him a bastard. I was the first aggressor and he was the aggrieved. So why did he spare me?

Even his envy was justified – I was clearly better off in life than he was and on top of that I was also friends with a girl down a highly coveted lane. In the context of that era in a middle class neighborhood, I was gold-plated……….

In the final analysis, his envy had merely pushed him into calling me James Bond and like an absolute nitwit I had rejected that undeserved compliment with a vile viciousness. How foolish.

Who knows we may have become friends. But no, his turning his back on me at the exam centre that day was like a story without a beginning coming to an end.

SUMMER OF '69

It floats like magic, a shimmering spread,
There in the distant past,
The dream we were weaving with golden thread
When something fell apart.

The summer of '69! My summer of '69!

Do all of us have defining seasons in our lives? Seasons whose redolence remains with us like the wetness in our eyes or the murmur of words in long lost diaries. I think we do. I know for sure that for me, the summer of '69 was one such.

Many things came together that summer. And something fell apart.

My college had just closed for vacations after the first year exams. The holidays were long and so I could very easily spend my leisure both at home (Patna) as well as in distant Purnea from where my cousins beckoned.

Cousins!

Who does not know the value of cousins, especially during "the growing years"! They are our friends, our confidants, our kindred souls. They do not sit in judgment, they do not admonish, they do not ever say NO. They simply take you in their warm embrace and make you feel good and wanted. They nourish you-and-yourself like nothing else in the world. And on top of it all, if you are in your late teens - tall, dark and some-some with vibrant hair and awakening flames – and your cousins are named Kiran, Rita, Nanhi, Tunni, Chandni, Sangeeta and Shelley, and you are headed towards them with not a care, then the world simply becomes one whizzing stream of happiness.

We were nine of us that summer. Sanjay and I were the only boys. We were under the care, roof and hospitality of one of the dearest uncle-aunt combinations one can ever hope to come across. The uncle was handsome, dapper, sharp, exciting, liberal. The aunt was matronly, soft, round, dimpled, yielding. While he encouraged us to be what we were, she kept doing things to remind us that we were no matter what, her children, who needed to be fed and looked after! As I said, they made an unmatchable match – Mauleshwar *Chacha* and *Chachi*.

The strange thing about that unforgettable summer is that nothing happened which could be defined as spectacular. Normally there are incidents which stand out prominently in our memory and they end up defining a phase in our lives. But no matter how much I tickle my brain, I cannot explain why that summer has remained so deeply etched in my consciousness. Probably it was simply that we were, so many of us, together under the same roof, all in our teens or thereabouts, and so completely inter-connected. I so clearly remember the clean, straight and unbroken line of our happiness. Surely it was our bounding joy that brushed the breeze that blew that summer and not the other way around.

It was a summer of awakening.

No matter what many might say, there is something unique about the bonding between male and female cousins, especially when they are coming of age. It's not just brother-sister, it's also boy-girl, grey-white, unsaid-unspoken….

And it was of course a summer of bonding.

The nine of us used to spend hours and hours, from earliest mornings to latest nights, doing things together – stories, spying, dark room, fancy dress, songs, jokes, or simply chatting and chatting and even more chatting. We had favorites of the day and we would fight for places next to them. When we fought the rest of us did all we could to patch things up. We made up fast because we were desperate to do so. We were that summer at least, each others' best friends forever. Nothing could break us.

And then one day…the "summer of '69" came to an abrupt end. It had to but it need not and should not have ended the way it did. We were somewhere…lying on our stomachs, our legs in the air, chatting in hushed tones in the cool of a high

ceilinged room.....who can remember such
details....I can't....I am simply drawing from a
hundred different fenced images of that unforgettably
happy summer....But wherever we were, whatever
we were doing, there gate-crashed into that huddled
togetherness, the shrill ring of the telephone.

I was plucked out. I knew by the look on my
Chachi's face that bad news awaited me.. It was my
father on the phone. Even in those difficult moments
for him, his voice was full of concern for me. He
informed me that my *Dadi* had passed away.

When I was very small, I used to call my
Dadi, *"Dada"*! Right from my earliest memories till
the day I left home to join college - be it winter,
spring, summer or fall - I used to sleep next to my
grandmother on the inner verandah of our home in
Patna. When I was small and afraid of the dark, I
would wake her up in the middle of nights because
I wanted to pee. She would wake up instantly to my
whispered *"Dada"* and then talk to me softly while
I stood on the edge of the verandah, watching the
silver curve streaming down in the moonlight. I was
a naughty child and later a difficult youngster. But
Dadi never left my side. She was always there for
me – as my savior and forgiver. I like to believe that
I was her favorite grandson and the memory of her
passing still casts a shadow over the bright days and
happy faces of that distant summer.

What a summer it was: a chorus of delight-filled
shouts petering out in hushed tones and scattered

sobs; lifelong bonds getting indelibly marked by the ink of death – in just a matter of weeks.

As the train sped through the night, it left behind a pattern of loops and turns that had very little to do with youthful innocence and the myth that life is all about straight lines, happiness, love, promises, friendship and……. cousins.

Some of us sensed this that night when we parted and in the process lost something forever. We grew up.

THE SMELL OF FLOWERS

Back we went, looking for him
In the darkness groping,
Guilt to wash and things to wish
In the darkness hoping,
His footprints I saw faintly in the sand,
The lingering smell of flowers in my hand.

I belong to the "Senior Cambridge" generation. And it is with pride that I say this, not only because it sounds good but also because the Christian missionary schools that offered this course those days were generally good schools. My own school at Patna - St. Xavier's - was one such.

In Senior Cambridge, English Language and Hindi were of course the two compulsory subjects – however, (perhaps) to be fair to students whose mother tongue was not Hindi, there was an alternative option called "Lower" Hindi!

My school was not only extremely well-rounded, it was also, at times and on occasions, a very kind school! And so it was that back benchers like me, whose mother tongue was Hindi and nothing but Hindi, were also allowed to opt for the easier variety!

This small narrative is about the Lower Hindi teacher for my Senior Cambridge batch – Mr. Francis Roberts. Mr. Roberts (mirthfully referred to as "Hitler") hailed from somewhere in North Bihar. He was dark complexioned, he plastered his hair down with oil, his large ears were bushier than his eyebrows and he sported a small square-shaped moustache over his upper lip! But the harder he tried to look and behave like a villain, the more he made us laugh.

Partho, a class-mate, was a devil. He was also daring. Once, when Mr. Roberts was walking up and down the aisle, intent on teaching us *sandhi-vichhed*, every time he went past Partho, the fellow ran a delicate and dexterous piece of chalk across the seat of Mr. Roberts' trousers. After several passes, Mr. Roberts' navy blue trousers, if not Mr. Roberts himself, had been successfully labeled. The hapless teacher could not figure out why the class kept sniggering whenever he turned his back until of course he had returned to the staff room and the offending label had been read out him!

If anyone, Partho was the "IDIOT", not Mr. Roberts.

Ming, a boy of Chinese descent, was the betting king in our Lower Hindi class. One winter day he snared some of us into a bet. The only precondition was that Mr. Roberts should come to school in his oft-worn full-sleeved jerkin. And that very day he did. So after class, we walked up to Mr. Roberts, pretending to seek clarity about something. And while we were going through this pretense, Ming suddenly caught hold of the zipper of Mr. Roberts' jerkin and said, *"Kya smart jerkin hai sir!"* and so saying, pulled the zipper down in one motion. Stunned, Mr. Roberts looked down at his unzipped jerkin and hastily tried to pull the zipper back. All of us stared in astonishment at the bare and hairy chest of Mr. Roberts.

Ming won the bet of course. He had always claimed that Mr. Roberts did not wear anything under his jerkin.

Dear and poor Mr. Roberts – we did so many unkind things to him with total impunity.

After we had written our Senior Cambridge exams, we got our traditional farewell dinner which was hosted by the school. The *padres* and all the teachers dined with us for the first and last time. Our coming of age was symbolized by the cigarettes that were allowed post dinner! It was an occasion and ritual which made many non-smokers light up too. And then, sooner than we could have ever imagined, our ten years in school simply went up in smoke.

We went around in somber groups, to take our formal leave of all the men and women who had in some way or the other touched and tinted our lives. No one was with me when I was taking leave of Mr. Roberts. I asked him, "Sir, any advice for me?" I could see that he was very pleased I had sought him out. He held me with both hands and replied. "Son, don't drink, don't smoke and don't dance." I suppose by his last piece of wisdom he meant that I should not run after girls!

After leaving school, my friends and I went our different ways. I went to Calcutta, some went to Delhi and a handful stayed behind at Patna to pursue higher studies. But we caught up with each other during our holidays. The wider world gives us a better perspective of our school-going days and so it happened with me and my friends too. We grew up quickly. One summer break, while we were reminiscing in the India Coffee House, just a year or two after having passed out of school, we realized that all of us now saw Mr. Roberts as he always was – a simple, modest and honest human being, craving for respect from his students. On an impulse we decided to visit him to pay our respects and wash some of our terrible guilt away. We found out where he lived, bought a flower bouquet and called on him one evening.

His lodgings were very modest – somewhere off Boring Canal Road. We stood on his dark verandah and knocked. He opened the door. He was wearing a *lungi* and a singlet. When he realized who we were, he got totally flustered. He did not know whether to invite us in or not. "*Arre aap log! Aise achanak. Aiyye….lekin.* But wait its cooler outside. Just give me two minutes." He left us standing there and went back in.

After some time Mr. Roberts returned. He was wearing a shirt over his *lungi* now.

"Sit down, sit down," he said, "why are you people standing. It's such an honour. Let me switch the light on." The low wattage bulb threw shadows all around us. There were four wooden chairs on the verandah, one with a broken arm rest. We, including Mr. Roberts were five in number.

"I will arrange for something. I will get some refreshments. Please sit. Please wait." He mumbled, he fumbled and again disappeared inside.

We looked at each other and knew we had made a big mistake. So leaving the flowers behind, we quietly slinked away – wordlessly like broken promises. As we melted into the night, it was a relief to hide from each other and from ourselves in the surrounding darkness.

However I carried back with me the lingering smell of flowers in my hand – like memories of simple men who leave the faintest of foot-prints on the sands of time.

TWO SNAPSHOTS

Amma shawled in the kitchen,
Papa in High-Court stripes,
Yashi-Vikram sweet as milk,
Followed by teenager types.
Must translate these albums now,
Name them Picture-Perfect,
Though past imperfect may have been,
Those joys we need not suspect.

The white-robed *Acharya* Rajneesh sits cross-legged under the small *bel* tree in our Exhibition Road precincts in a comfortable chair and speaks. He has large, mesmeric eyes and his nasal voice with the peculiar accent floats soothingly over the assembly of men and women who sit on *durries* which have been spread on the ground. I watch him from a distance. I am at once drawn to his engaging personality and repelled by his scented white robe and designer *chappals*.................

Bari Amma who was always drawn towards a larger sweep of things – she was politically inclined and at one time was even a Member of the Legislative Council – had turned determinedly to social work and philosophy after the premature death of *Babuji* in 1964. She was a rationalist and an avid student of contemporary thought and thereby had come in touch with *Acharya* Rajneesh who was beginning to make a name for himself through his discourses on spirituality. She had invited him to come to Patna and speak and engage with the townspeople. Perhaps she was looking for some peace of mind for herself too. I had started to have a mind of my own by now and when Rajneesh opened himself to answering questions, I too raised my hand. Thankfully he did not look towards me because my heart was thumping wildly at the prospect of speaking in front of so many people – I was and continue to be acutely shy. My question therefore remained unrevealed. Just the previous day, I had cornered *Bari Amma* by demanding to know why the house-guest (yes he stayed in our home during his Patna visit) had to dress in a stereotype robe and grow his hair long when he kept preaching that to free one's mind one had to free oneself of all conventions. Why was he not practicing what he preached – why the robe and the pendant, why the self acquired suffix to his name? Why was he dressing himself like a *guru* when he was asking people to be independent and not to follow? *Bari Amma* heard me wordlessly and asked me to ask the man himself. That day, ten yards away from the *bel* tree under which the neo-Buddha sat, I got the chance to corner him but I blew it.

(The rest is history – the *Acharya* caught the imagination of the "flower generation" through his mouth-salivating philosophy of *Sambhog Se Samadhi* – Enlightenment through Copulation – *Acharya* Rajneesh swiftly became *Bhagwan* Rajneesh and then before *Bari Amma* could wipe the dust off her spectacles, he became OSHO and was (reportedly) the 4th largest land owner in the U.S.A.)

He used to write to *Bari Amma* on 5-paisa post-cards when they first corresponded and referred to her as "Sushilaji". The day she received a communication from him starting with "Priya Sushila" on scented paper, she threw the letter away. And thus was consigned to the waste basket by my family, the man who would be God!

* * *

Its 1974.. I am studying Business Management at XLRI and Sheel *Bhaiya* the banker, is getting married to his sweetheart at Calcutta. I am home (summer vacation), my summer project is with the Bata Shoe Factory at Digha (suburb), and the house is abuzz with marriage arrangements. The whole family (sans *Babuji* and *Dadi* who passed away five years after *Babuji*) is gathered at Exhibition Road. The *raunaq* is back in my beloved home and life is happy once again!

Some one comes clattering into the drawing room. "She is back, she is back!" The animated chit-chat in the room comes to an abrupt end.

I am off my chair and run after the excited person before anyone can even ask who is back. I rush into the rear verandah and there in the court-yard near the *bawarchi-khana*, is she!

Burhia Dai! - toothless, grinning from one long ear to another, wearing a bright yellow *sari* and tears streaking down her wrinkled face. She can hardly speak. I am joyous and so is the family which now stands beside me, looking down at her and laughing, exclaiming, questioning..........

Burhia Dai was old and known as *Burhia Dai* even when we (the five boys at Exhibition Road) were in our knickers and perhaps even running around naked on occasions in the inner court-yard and bathing under the tap where the utensils used to be washed on a large stone slab! She was our "maid" and Yashi for sure spent a major portion of his infancy straddling her bony waist. She was a smoker and the sweet smell of the *hookah* always hung about her. She looked after us with the fierceness of an aging cat but at the same time she was not beyond using abusive language and bawdy stories to get her point across! One of the male servants once taught us a verse and asked us to address the same to *Burhia Dai*. He was settling his own score with her for sure but what did we care? The verse went like this:

jawan ho ya burhia, nanhi si ho gudia,
phir bhi ye aurat zehar ki hai pudia...

(be she young or old,
or be she just a doll
yet she, no matter what,
will ever be a moll..)

That first time it was as if someone had lit the fuse of a *Diwali pataka* under *Burhia Dai*. She simply took off – she raged and chased and yes she abused.

"Isn't your grandmother old, is your mother not a woman? Go and repeat that to them. Get out, get away you scoundrels. Who taught you this? Tell me his name and I will show him what a woman's poison is….." she raged. We ran away laughing. We knew we had a new-found weapon and used it many times thereafter even though she never did us any harm.

Every six months or so, a neat looking man, short and dour, with a pencil moustache, thin lips and slicked back hair, used to visit her. He always wore a starched half sleeved shirt over a crisp white *dhoti*. *Burhia Dai* would hand over her six months' wages quietly to him. He would not even have the time to sit with her in her sweet smelling room – mother and son would thus simply stand and converse for a few minutes and then he would walk away, looking neither left nor right!

As we grew older we became more and more attached to her and if not attached, more and more appreciative of her loyalty and selflessness. She, wrinkled, bent, happy and now even in the habit of muttering to herself, kept pace with us. Then one day, much like Forrest Gump, she just stopped and announced, "I think I'll go home now." Her native village was somewhere near Motihari and so after the passing of a whole generation she picked up her life's possessions (a slim cloth bundle) and went away....

But now she was back in a bright yellow *sari* and crying and telling us she heard Sheel *Babu* was getting married and this was her home not some god-forsaken village in Motihari....she kept babbling even as we dispersed smiling and happy to have her back in our midst once again. The smell of the *hookah* and the strains of the *shehnai* inter-twined and floated effortlessly though the house.

Burhia Dai died a year or two later. She died in the Exhibition Road house.....in her home.

THE MADNESS OF THE SANE

Do not try to clip my wings
And do not shut the door on me,
For then I'll swerve and I will swing,
The madness of the sane you'll see.

Sometime in 1974, when I was home during a short break from XLRI, I heard about the "Rajendranagar" girls – several of my school mates were in Patna pursuing Medicine and they were friendly with a girl called Neelam (with whom they were rubbing shoulders at the University) – Neelam lived with her family in Rajendranagar – her family had a father, a brother and several sisters of varying ages, she being the second eldest.

I was naturally curious and keen, so my friend Sitangshu took me to her house in his scooter one day.

We stopped in front of a neat double storyed structure with a well lit verandah and a patch of green in front. A low boundary wall ran around the house. It was dark outside.

Neelam was there and so were several others scattered on the stoop and grass. One of them was perched on the wall between their house and their neighbour's. The light from the verandah settled on them in soft, hazy tones. While I was still being introduced by Sitangshu, the girl on the boundary wall jumped down and ran indoors – I just got a glimpse as she flashed through the verandah – of a fair complexioned girl in a long printed skirt and a bright red top……

Throughout that distracted, scented evening on the patch of green at 16-A Rajendrnagar, I kept hoping that the girl in the skirt would come out. But she didn't. Even as early as the ride back home with Sitangshu, I knew that I wanted to marry that girl. Sitangshu informed me that her name was Poonam.

The thought and the image of the girl in the long skirt consumed me. I did not have time. I would have to leave for Jamshedpur within a few days. So without a moment's hesitation I confided in my friends. Neelam was taken into confidence too. The very next day I was back at 16-A Rajendranagar. The drawing room where I sat alone and waiting had blue and yellow walls. A large, garlanded photograph of a very simple looking lady leaned forward from one of the walls with a smile. Just then Poonam walked in – she wore a sari and I noticed that her face looked severely scrubbed – it was devoid of any make-up. She had large, very large eyes.

Small and petite, she leaned back in her sofa like a child and listened to me wordlessly. I have this habit of coming to the point swiftly and abruptly – therefore not surprisingly I found myself professing my love to her soon after she had been sent into the room by her elder sister. Her silence and reluctance to meet my eye made me desperate and I quickly clarified to her that I was not just desirable of making her my girl-friend but that I looked upon her as someone who I would like to marry as soon as I could stand on my own.

Well, persistence paid. We became a pair. Soon enough my two years at XLRI were up and I was picked up from the campus by Asian Paints to become a Management Trainee. The final exams ended sometime in April and the appointment letter from Asian Paints asked me to join them at Bombay from the 2nd of June.

The prospect of a minimum year long separation from Poonam killed everything around me and the world became for me the most desolate place on earth! Poonam was far more practical and tried her best to shoo my unhappiness away. But I wanted to get engaged to her before leaving.

Poonam's sisters were a plenty, I was the 'incoming brother-in-law' and therefore I foresaw no problem. As I saw it, Neelam (married now) who was thankfully in Patna, would explain the situation to her father and ask him to visit my father and seek the 'alliance'. My parents were in any case waiting for this eventual eventuality. Such was the inviolable convention those days.

But Neelam said NO she would not stick her neck out because her husband did not want her "to get involved"! Neerja, the eldest was not in Patna. The rest (Manjari, Anjali, Tanuja) were younger and therefore not qualified for such a task. Mukul, the brother was blissfully oblivious and that I thought was as it should be!

So then I asked Poonam to talk to her father. She dillied. Then she dallied. Days flew past. Panic gripped me. Finally, I squared up and confronted Poonam. She looked back with tears in her eyes. She could not do it. She did not want to be a bad example to her younger sisters!

What? Bad example? Matlab? How? I mean how bad example??????

Try to understand my pitiable state and pardon me. Because the very next day after those big fat tears, I actually walked up to my father and requested him to call on Mr. Nandkishore Prasad (Poonam's father) and tell him that he, my father, wanted to make his, Poonam's father's daughter, his, my father's, daughter-in-law! (Yes I was babbling by now!)

Even Papa, the kindest of men, when thus confronted, looked at his son witheringly and shook his head sadly. His eyes seemed to ask, 'have I actually sired this fellow?'

Please get the picture because you must.

The month of May is getting licked by a moth..... the glaze in my eyes is turning opaque..... the sleeve of my shirt is being tugged by a madman.........for how else can you explain how the following happened?

I informed my father with rare sullenness that I would drop him to the High Court because I would need the car. He did not question. By around 10.45 the car and I were back home. Then I started pacing and rehearsing. Finally at around 1.00, I took a deep breath, got behind the wheel and drove off. My destination – the office of the Chief Engineer PWD (Poonam's father) which I had been told was in a building near the Old Secretariat in the New Capital Area. At 1.15 I parked the car in the dusty compound of a building so heavily windowed that it looked like a bee-hive. At 1.20 I was inside the annex leading to the Chief Engineer's office. The man sitting behind his type-writer looked up. On inquiry he told me that 'engineer saheb' had just left for his home for lunch. 'Just' he said, 'just'. He even pointed in the direction from which, moments ago I had come.

I was unstoppable by now - in the zone - hooked, booked, fried and cooked. I rushed out and saw the cream colored Ambassador I knew so well (BRP 5779) driving off. I ran to my car....

And thus, on an unsuspecting summer afternoon, down the famous Bailey Road of Patna, there started a chase to remember. Near the Patna

Women's College the road was maddeningly cluttered by rickshaws because the college had just disgorged its highly coveted contents in a riot of colors and sounds. But I coveted none at the time, in fact I cursed all of them because they were holding me up and allowing the Chief Engineer to get away. But drivers who have cut their teeth in the by-lanes of Patna know how to weave through rickshaws, bicycles, girls and cattle. I was out of the mess in no time and roaring away. The black road snaked and slithered frighteningly into and under me even as my eyes remained glued on the shimmering car in the narrowing distance. The traffic became denser as I neared the Dak-Bungalow Road/Fraser Road crossing. I had been zipping recklessly but now I had to slow down. Yet I was gaining, yard by precious yard. But just when I was in striking distance, the driver of the other car suddenly decided to become an adversary. He stepped on his accelerator and started to pull away.

Challenged and stung I honked like crazy and zigzagged but with the intent of an arrow. And then, the adrenalin oozing like sweat, when I knew the moment had arrived, I delivered the *coup-de-grace* with an expertly executed spurt, swing and jam. Directly in front of Roshan Brothers my car lurched to a halt with BRP 5779 trapped hopelessly in its shuddering wake. The Chief Engineer's car had been forced into a screeching halt too. I surged out, banged the door of my car behind me and ran to the rear of the trapped car. Its window rolled down and I saw Poonam's father, cool as a cucumber, staring at me with consternation. He recognized me of course.

My trance came to an end there and then. The enormity and absurdity of my behavior hit me. I managed to greet him and stuttered my way into telling him that I wanted to speak to him about his daughter. At best he batted an eyelid. He then said he was going home for lunch and added with mild asperity that he thought his office would be a better meeting place. He looked at his watch and asked me if 3.30 was fine by me. Dazed, I nodded my head.

"Chalo bhai" I thought I heard him say. Dumbly, I watched the window go up and his car shrug away.

The concluding part of the exchange happened on schedule at 3.30. I was more a punctured tube than hot wheels by then. He was as cool and kind as he always was.

As a consequence Poonam's father called on my father on the 28th of May. I got engaged to her on the 29th. And on the 30th I left home for distant Bombay to start my career.

As for my late father-in-law……he was such a good man. He never mentioned a word about the car chase to me – never ever. But on many occasions I did catch him looking at me when he thought I was not looking…..he always had that uncertain, doubtful look on his face - you know the kind of expression you have when you stop in your tracks and peer into the dark because you think a shadow had just crossed your path?

THE CJ's BUNGALOW

Never in tune with the aces,
Badly dressed I looked a tramp,
From tea, biscuits and smiling faces,
I emerged a bedraggled champ.
Taken to court, I lowered my head,
My spirit was up, the world well-fed.

It surprises me to this day as to why I always fell so short of the family average in the way I dressed. And this is particularly true of my school, college and early career days. You just have to look at old photographs for evidence. I stood out like a sore thumb for my sartorial deviance!

Why? Because my best friend (Samma) was the son of the repair-wala across the road? But I had a whole family just a stone's throw from where I used to be most times, to guide me, to set my belt right, to order me to polish my scuffed shoes and tie my laces, to comb my hair, to tuck the shirt, to ensure that my shorts fell straight and not at crazy angles... And my family did its best too….but to no avail. Let us just say that I was incurable.

I improved as I grew older but during my early career days also, I was a source of anxiety and sometimes derision because of the carelessness and absence of taste I exhibited through my clothes.

I once wore an indigo blue shirt and chocolate brown trousers to a party. The host and my friend (Balbir) looked me up and down. His better-half (Kaval) looked me up and down. Both shook their heads, beckoned Poonam (my wife) and looked at her, askance. She in turn looked at me askance and pretended as if she was seeing me for the first time that day! She too shook her head and then the three walked away. Just like that! I must have cut a sorry figure, standing by myself, nursing my drink and bruised ego!

I am better now, much better I am told. But those days I was a badly dressed guy.

Gauhati. Early 1980s.

My parents visiting me for the first time after my marriage and after my having started off in life and having set up my own home! It's a memory I shall cherish till my days are over. My wife quaked (unnecessarily) with the responsibility and I basked (rightfully) in the glow which came our way because my father by then had become a High Court Judge.

The protocol was that a visiting (even on a holiday) high court judge went calling on the Chief Justice of the High Court of the place being visited. So an appointment was taken and on the appointed day (must have been a Saturday or a Sunday, both being off days for any High Court), I drove my parents to the Chief Justice's bungalow.

The drive-way inside the gates was long, well tended and winding. I was directed into the portico. A liveried *chapraasi* with ornamental head gear opened the doors. I informed my father that I would join them after parking the car.

The same tall gentleman with the head gear showed me, with the wave of his hand, where (in the distance, near a clump of trees) I could park my vehicle. In the rear view mirror, I saw my parents dissolving into the folds of the Chief Justice's bungalow.

This is when the fun began! I parked my good old Ambassador and got out. In so doing I revealed my fully attired five-foot-ten self to whoever was watching. And, (you guessed it right), it was immediately assumed by all such, that I was the chauffeur, the pilot, the driver – whatever I chose to choose!

No sooner I realized what was actually happening, I started to enjoy myself, especially because those of the staff who had assumed what I was not, were very friendly. I was taken to a secluded area behind the trees. I could see this was where the staff quarters were. There was a wooden bench and I was invited to sit on it. With remarkable swiftness someone returned with a cup of tea and two biscuits. The cup was in a saucer and the biscuits were in the hand. They were deposited on the bare bench on which I sat. I was urged to eat and drink and these I did with absolute gladness. Apart from the tea and biscuits, everything about the whole experience was very sweet too. I remember engaging in random talk with the man who was playing host. The breeze was cool and the trees around me swayed with a sense of camaraderie and brotherhood.........as Wodehouse would have said – "all was well with the world"!

But it was not!

Back in the sitting room of the Chief Justice's bungalow there was concern and consternation. More than my father, my mother started to wonder where her son was. Why was he taking so long to park the car?

"I wonder where Raj is," she finally said.

And thus, unknown to me, as the saying goes, I was finally out of the bag.

Soon after, someone came running to the idyllic world where I was. The peace was shattered by a riot of reactions which included, not in any particular order, shouts, accusations, apologies, appeals and a scramble to return me to where I belonged. In all this I was made to feel, one after the other, two different entities - now I was an unwanted bundle, now I was a chest of gold, now I was a tramp and now I was a prince....

I was finally led into the plush confines of the CJ's bungalow. Before anymore commotion could restart, I cut everything and everybody short with a straight untruth.

"I was admiring the trees and the flowers," I explained.

My mother saw through me, my father stared at me and the Chief Justice and his wife kept their eyes focused on what I wore and how I looked while retaining their composure with remarkable restraint. I nodded, I greeted, I smiled, I shuffled…At last the richly upholstered sofa to which I was directed, sucked me in and I was very relieved with the obscurity it provided.

After the pleasant chit-chat I had just had under the sway of trees, I found the measured conversation on jurisprudence between the two older men, dreary and uninteresting. I turned my attention to the two ladies but they offered no relief either – I had no desire to join them on a visit to the Kamakhya Temple…..So after my second cup of tea, I excused myself and sauntered out to the sweeping verandah which the sitting room led out to. I stood transfixed by the view it afforded.

Hardly a hundred yards from me, flowed the mighty Brahmaputra. And such a majestic sight it was!

The roar of the river reached me like the whisper of the wise – I flow because I go, I go because I flow, it said….a great sense of continuity seemed to settle all over me… Presently I turned to go back inside. And back within me was the happy feeling that all was well with the world after all!

MRS. ATAL

In the days when I lived a wonderful life,
A thousand deaths one day I died –
With an office car and a pretty wife,
Why by the roadside was I spied,
Pumping the tyres of a bike that wobbled,
By pretty Mrs. A, all lipsticked and goggled!

I will ever be grateful to Gauhati. One of the happiest phases of my life was spent there. I was very young in my career. I was the Branch Manager of Asian Paints with a full-fledged Sales Office-cum-Depot under me. I had a Company car and I had a pretty wife. Cream on this cake, I had a handful of friends, all Branch Managers in different companies, all married and all with pretty wives. Every week-end was party time and every once in a quarter or two, we, the Branch Managers "jointly" covered by road our common sales territory (the seven North East States) through one of the most scenic landscapes in the country. The North East flung its arms out far and wide over hills and across forests. The long undulating road routes between towns were interspersed by quaint villages and townships where mud huts had neatly tended flower beds fronting them and *"nukkads"* had young men focussed around carrom boards placed on improvised platforms....

I could go on and on to sketch that picturesque region and profile those invaluable friends. What an eclectic group we were! With pride and gratitude I would introduce you to Ratan and Rajni Kaul who were so kind and hospitable. My first fridge and first whisky happened because of Ratan. I would take you to the gracious and learned Balbir and Kaval Bhasin. It was from Balbir that I learnt that Robert Browning, not W H Auden, wrote "The Last Ride Together"! If you were seeking high quality sound and western music, I would take you to the aesthetes, Sudhir and Pratibha Rao. And from there we would all troop to the bungalow of the ever welcoming Nandu and Praveena Pillai. You may not believe it but Nandu learnt driving while he drove us over the climbing, winding *ghats* of Meghalaya in his spanking new Ambassador car! That day we died a thousand deaths......but those days we lived a wonderful life.

Till one day, there appeared on the distant horizon, one Mrs Atal. Her husband (Mr Atal I presume), was the Manager of M/S Carritt Moran & Company, the high profile tea broking firm. Because "tea auction" was a big commercial activity, the fact that she was the wife of the Manager of Carritt Moran, placed her on a natural pedestal! And as it so happens in such cases, she was also extremely beautiful. During club nights or similar social gatherings, my eyes would always get drawn towards her and no amount of ribbing from my friends or icy arrows from my wife would arrest my restless eyes... ..I was afflicted – my equilibrium was disturbed!

Those were early days of the Assam agitation – not many may know but the United Liberation Front of Assam (ULFA) of today was preceded by the milder All Assam Students' Union (AASU) then. My tenure in Gauhati coincided with the spectacular and sudden emergence of the AASU. *Bandhs, morchas* and sporadic violence and intimidations quickly became a way of life. "Outsiders" felt threatened at times and most Corporate Managers like us had to draw up highly confidential documents detailing the steps to be taken, including evacuation of staff and families, in case circumstances forced us to shut down operations in the region.

It was the peak of summer I remember. There was a call for a total Assam *bandh* that day. But I had to go to office for sometime at least to attend to something very urgent. Taking out the car was fraught with danger. Only essential and emergency services vehicles had the permission to ply.

Walking all the way to Rehabari (office) from Christian Basti on G.S. Road (residence), especially in that heat, was the last alternative. Then I remembered that the landlord's young son had a mournful looking bicycle gathering dust under the staircase. I sought permission which was unhesitatingly granted. I wore a shabby pair of trousers over a careless shirt, dusted the bicycle seat, waved jauntily to my highly concerned wife and wobbled off to office. The road was wide and clear. The legs were young and energetic. The sun was big and hot. In no time at all I was sweating like a pig and struggling. Was I getting old so soon? Why was the bicycle moving so slowly in spite of my muscled efforts? Nonplussed, I got off my vehicle. I cursed. Both tyres were almost flat. Since I had covered almost half the distance, there was no question of turning back. So I started pushing the two wheeled piece of junk up the largely deserted road, hoping to find help. I had hardly covered fifty meters when I spotted a couple of cycle-tyres hanging from a horizontal pole up head. I had seen land from my sea of despair.

The repair-*wala* was an old man. I did not have to say a word. Smiling toothlessly, he creaked out of his shaded perch and asked me to hold the nozzle of the rubber pipe to the wheel-spout while he worked the air-pump. As I watched him I could see that he was almost literally breathing his life into the nearly lifeless tyre. This was not right. I got up, squared my shoulders and asked the old man to hand over the pump to me. I started pumping with a vengeance.......

And then into that sweat-dripping swishing silence there came a distant sound. I looked up and sideways. Something white was shimmering down the coal-tarred road. It swiftly transformed into a speeding Fiat which slowed down to a crawl directly in front of me. The tinted glass rolled down. And who and what should I see but the stunning Mrs. Atal staring straight at me and myself, pumping *hava* by the roadside into the limp tyre of a crippled bicycle….. A withering look, a haughty turn of the head, the roar of engines and she was gone….

I pictured her picturing me. Unstoppable sweat flowed out, my thick curly hair turned lank and my unseeing eyes drilled holes into the nothingness of despair. My plight, my self-pity and my very existence on that hot and humid day, smote me. I prayed for the sun to melt my disgusting self or for wretched earth to do me a *Sita Maiyya*………I died.

My memory fails me beyond that…. However, I must have quickly recovered from my malady and I must have lived happily ever after. But I must certainly not have told this ego-puncturing tale to my friends and wife!!

I am telling you now…..

FLYING FIRST

It was a windswept field I saw
And a grassy dome,
A lone Dakota in the grey,
I heard its plaintive drone.
And years later an orange ticket
And a letter home.

This is of the time when a person's first flight was an 'event'.

It was awaited with both excitement and anxiety - in that order. But as the D day drew nearer, the order got reversed. And in case your near and dear ones were not on hand to see your terrified face before you boarded, you wrote to them about it. It was a rite of passage for those of my generation. Before that, many or most middle class people never flew and after it, flying was no big deal. But as I said, once upon a time, it was.

My first flight happened after I started working. I joined my first organisation at Bombay (train) and my first posting was to Ahmedabad (again frustratingly train). Both these train journeys had been by 'first class' and this in itself was not a bad consolation those days.

But thankfully my much awaited and anticipated first flight materialized soon after. I was the Assistant Branch Manager and my boss, naturally, the Branch Manager. These Branch Managers (much senior in age, though not in wisdom) were being slowly replaced by young brats like me (MBAs) in Asian Paints those days. Therefore for all important meetings at Head Quarters (Bombay) both the Manager and his young assistant were being asked to attend. And this happy situation led to my being handed over my first air-ticket. I quickly dashed off a letter home with the news that my first flight was going to take place on such and such a date. Alas there were no mobile phones and digital cameras then – else that shiny orange ticket would have lived on.

My boss was kind enough to let me have the window seat ("oh it's your first flight is it" he had laughed). The short flight from Ahmedabad to Bombay was fascinating – I experienced no fear or sickness. The air-hostesses were a dream come true and so were so many other things, including the toffees which were so smilingly offered. Like a seasoned veteran I was careful to pick up just one! (Only later was I to realize that this was one of the first signs of a first timer!)

We landed. With the smile and shrug of a veteran I got up and followed my boss out of the plane's dazzling door. Back on terra-firma, while still under the giant silver wings, I surveyed the world around me with benevolence, took out a cigarette and lit up.

What happened next is not a happy memory. Shouts, abuses, admonitions followed. My cigarette and match box were snatched away. But the most cutting and unkindest memory is of a uniformed attendant asking me loudly "THIS IS YOUR FIRST FLIGHT OR WHAT" and my boss confirming mirthfully that yes it was....

* * *

But on the subject of 'first flights' the cake very definitely goes to Yashi, my younger brother. His happened just a few years after mine. He was working for the State Bank of India and was posted at Ranchi. He was in Patna on some work (I was home on leave) and had, after some persuasion, decided to fly back instead of taking the overnight train. We were living in 3 Polo Road - the airport was quite close by – so close that we could hear the planes landing and taking off. Thankfully, the flights in and out of Patna were very few those days.

Yashi's flight was at 10.00 in the morning. Papa normally left for the High Court at 10.00. The transportation scheduling became easy therefore – the car would reach Yashi to the airport and come back well in time to take Papa to the High Court.

Times had progressed and hence the entire family was not going to the airport to see Yashi off.

Since I was a veteran flier by now, the mantle fell on me. I took on the assignment of launching my brother off on his first flight.

Yashi took his leave of everyone (now gathered on the verandah) after the customary spoon of *dahi-cheeni* for safe travel. He and I then got into the car and left. We reached the airport in ten minutes. At the yet-to-be-opened check-in counter we were informed by an official that the flight was delayed by one hour. There was no point in hanging around, so we decided to return home. The car could reach Papa to the High Court and have enough time to come back to once again take us to the airport.

Papa left for work before ten that day.

"*Gaadi turant vapis le aana Shyam, airport jana hai,*" I shouted to the driver to make doubly sure that he had understood.

It was winter time, so all of us decided to sit out under the striped yellow garden-umbrella.

The daily coffee (served earlier than usual that day) and the roar of a landing aircraft reached us at the same time. It was just about ten minutes since my father had left with the car. I jumped up and so did Yashi. How could the flight have landed? Had we not been told that it was delayed by an hour? Soon all of us were in a panic. We did not have a vehicle with us. Polo Road was at one end of a secluded area of the city where only high ranking government officials resided in bungalows....

"Get a rickshaw," someone shouted.

One of the staff went running out of the gate to seek out one. It would not be easy – rickshaws were rare in this part of the city.

We finally got through to the airport (on phone) only to be confirmed that indeed the aircraft bound for Ranchi had landed and that the check-in counter would close shortly. Frustrated I protested into the mouth piece only to be told that the flight that was delayed was a different one, the Delhi bound one.

Polo Road was a C shaped tree lined lane – an off-shoot of Taylor Road which ran straight and wide towards the airport. One of the staff had run out of the main gate of our bungalow towards Taylor Road – now another went running out of the rear gate. But no rickshaw was found and none came. Panic and frustration made jumping jacks out of us. Accusations started to fly around – whose idea was it to come back from the airport? Did you make inquiries at the inquiry counter? How could that attendant have known that you were asking about the Ranchi flight?

A quiet voice suddenly silenced the cacophony surrounding us. It said, "Yashi Mama, hop on."

We looked in amazement at Suman (my nephew) and his bicycle. He was sitting in it in the drive-way and quietly asking Yashi to hop on behind him (on the carrier).

Less than a minute later the very same bicycle shot out of the gate and disappeared from sight. Riding it was a class X student of St. Michael's High

School and sitting pillion on it and praying to God was the banker, his air bag clutched clumsily across his heaving chest.

Never before and never since – I am absolutely sure of this – in the history of commercial aviation, has a man caught his first flight after reaching the airport as a pillion passenger on a rickety old bicycle.

This historic event went unrecorded but has finally claimed its place in this narrative. So let it be known, once and for all, that something as grounded as this also happened once upon a time on a cold winter's day in a small town in India, in the long and eventful history of man's rise on earth.

(Coincidentally, the phrase 'Flying First' is painted in bold letters on the roof of a hangar in one corner of the airfield at Ranchi – you can see it when you are landing there. How or why, I cannot say, but it's there – at least it used to be. So if you ever see it or come across it anywhere, you might be justified in thinking that you know where it came from!!!)

MY FATHER'S FRIEND

I think on the back steps of my home...
Every charminar in my hand
Was once a castle in the air
And this dry cough is the rattle
Of promises written in the sand...
Such is the descent in love-
From ivory throne
To these steps of stone.

You would not know, looking at his spare and bent physique, that he and his brother were famous tennis players of their time. He was also an ace swimmer and when my father was teaching me how to swim, he would tell me that the sign of a classic swimmer lay in how he swam underwater.

"Have you observed Jishu swimming underwater? He swims along the floor of the pool. That's the way to do it." Papa would then show me how to cut water under the surface. "If you master it, you will find still waters at the bottom where there is least turbulence and resistance." I could never become an ace swimmer so I don't know if technically Papa's assessment was correct or not. But the fact remained that Mr. Jishu Nandi was a sort of a legend in his time. He was a great ball-room dancer too and was much sought after by the ladies during the annual New Year's Ball at the Club. And yes, as you might think, he was also a bachelor! One abiding image is that of this neatly built man, in a dark double breasted suit, moving across a row of brightly attired, cross-legged ladies watching a tennis match on the lawns of the New Patna Club, greeting them, bowing to them and ordering refreshments for them to the uniformed "bearer" following him. Mr. Jishu Nandi was a dandy alright.

But as I grew out of the star-spangled world of childhood and stepped into the harsh light of day, Uncle Jishu was gradually left behind as a fading cut-out in my sub-conscious, much like peeling cinema posters on forgotten walls.

I left Patna after school for higher education and then I started working. And so it was that I next saw Uncle Jishu after a very long gap.

A few years into my professional life, I had changed my job to manage a posting to Patna. My office (Nerolac Paints) was situated on Bailey Road. The New Patna Club was just a short drive from there and since I was an avid tennis player, I managed a "tennis membership" for myself and started playing on its lush courts regularly. A local tennis tournament was going on. I was on one of the courts playing against a robust adversary. Chandrabhanu or Chandrakant was his name and he was giving me a torrid time. I had a fairly good forehand, I used to hit flat and hard and could make the ball skim the net. That day I was hitting well too. But to no avail. The blighter on the other side knew how to volley and all my grunt-laden shots were getting swatted back. My angled base-line fury was up against net-towering disdain and the latter was winning hands down, almost literally.

"You are giving him too much time. Don't allow him to come to the net."

I heard this while I was crouched well behind the baseline, ready to tackle Chandra's next serve. He served. I judged the trajectory of the ball, swiftly shuffled to the left, got into position, swung my Prince Pro racquet and slapped the ball back with a stinging forehand. Chandra was waiting at the net and he stop-volleyed my hard return with a dismissive smile. Frustrated, witless and helpless, I looked back.

And there he was – Uncle Jishu, in crushed white trousers, bush-shirt, afghan *chappals* and a hat ....he looked old and shrunken, much like the Charminar cigarette dangling between his fingers. His smile had a missing tooth. He was bent forward and he had one hand pressed against his stomach. He tagged with me to the other end of the base-line and advised me that my forehand, good no doubt, was useless against my adversary's volleying. Don't take so much time while returning his shots. Rush your returns by going forward to meet the ball so that he does not get the time to come to the net. Once you have him pinned to the back of his court, you can beat him on the strength of your better ground shots.

I thanked him and turned the match around into a more even one. During the course of the match, I kept looking out for Uncle Jishu but he was not to be seen. By the time my match ended, it was almost dark. I went home feeling relieved and grateful.

That day I inquired about him from my father and told him about my encounter on the tennis court.

"He looked very different," I added. "Not just old but different...."

"Oh, Jishu!" my father said shaking his head and left it at that. I looked at him but did not pursue the matter further.

Just about a week later, one evening, I was wading through a jumble of mails and files in my office when there was a hesitant knock. Nobody ever knocked on my door. My office colleagues did not and neither did the stray paint retailer visiting us to place a rare order. So the knock caught my attention. I looked up with curiosity and said "Come in."

"Raj?"

Uncle Jishu's face peeped from behind the half closed door. Surprised, I got up, stumbled around the table and opened the door for him. I welcomed him and sat him down. He seemed very hesitant and unsure, a far cry. I called for a cup of tea and pushed the ash-tray towards him and offered him a cigarette. He smiled then and nodded his head. He fumbled with the matches so I offered him a light. He had a deep, gravelly voice. He wanted to know the outcome of my tennis match that day.

"I won Uncle!" I lied. "I wanted to thank you." He smiled widely then and gave me some more tips on court-craft. As he relaxed and sipped his tea, I kept wondering why he had dropped in on me. We soon ran out of conversation but then he got up to leave. At the door he paused and seemed to look for something in his pockets. Then he turned and asked me if I could lend him some money since he had left his wallet behind.

"Of course Uncle, how much do you need?" I enquired, taking out my wallet.

"Oh twenty will do," he laughed, looking at the floor. "*Rickshaw* fares have shot up so much."

I watched him going down the stairs, one hand holding the railing, the other placed on the side of his stomach, a cigarette dangling from his flaky lips. Many thoughts raced through my mind – why did he hold his stomach like that all the while, didn't he have a car, shouldn't I have offered to drop him to his destination, shouldn't I have gone down the stairs with him…..

However these questions and indeed the man himself did not stay with me for long. I even forgot to mention his visit to my father that evening. But I did when just a few days later, Uncle Jishu came up to my office a second time. Again he accepted a cigarette from me and again before leaving he asked me if I could give him some money. And again I gave him twenty rupees.

Papa heard me out in silence. We were walking around our beloved rose garden at 3 Polo Road. He slowed down, lost in thoughts. Then he put his hand on my shoulder and said, "He is an old friend Raj." There was such gentleness in my father's voice that he did not have to say anything more or explain anything else.

It became a pattern – Uncle Jishu coming to my office, the two of us sharing small, inane talk over tea and cigarettes and the twenty rupees at the door. The frequency never changed – once a week – and once when I tried to hand over a hundred rupee note he put his tongue between his heavily stained teeth and shook his head.

Often, after he had left, I would stand at my office window overlooking Bailey Road and watch the sun go down. I would train my eyes on a distant building. It was fascinating to watch the shadows creep over its white structure. What stood tall and proud would almost fade into the gathering gloom in moments. I would shake my head at the irony of it all and wait for its first light to be lit. It always did and made me think of a smoke-shrouded cigarette glowing in the dark.

ONE DAY IN THE LIFE
OF A SALESMAN

They won't like to cross your path
If you are in Sales,
It is a mean street to walk,
Be it Warangal or Wales...

Manoj Chakravarti and I were on our way from Patna to Bhagalpur in a hired car. We were colleagues in Nerolac Paints. Dussehra was nearing and even though the festive season was in the air, we were on a serious business mission.

Dussehra / Diwali is the make or break season for the Paints business and Bhagalpur and its adjuncts had been enemy territory for some years. We had embarked upon our extended road trip earlier than usual because we wanted to pre-empt competition. In particular we were hoping to break the back of British (now Berger) Paints by getting into a deal with the wily Ishwar Babu (the biggest rascal and therefore not surprisingly, the largest paints retailer in that part of our country).

Bhagalpur is north of Patna and the road route takes you there via Mokameh Ghat. The double-decker bridge at Mokameh affords you a grand view of the Ganga flowing below and around. People make wishes and throw coins into the river from trains, cars, buses as they clang over its swollen waters. Both Manoj and I knew what prayers our respective coins would carry that day. They would be directed towards "Ishwar" for sure.

On the way, we made the conventional stop at Champapur which had become famous for its Mamta Hotel. Mamta was the watering hole for all motorists those days – it was bang on the roadside and depending on the weather, it gave you the option of sitting out in the open or in its cool interiors. Since it was early September we sat inside and ordered for *chhole bature* followed by its famous chilled *kheer* (which used to be served in fragrant *kaptees*).

We were about to finish our meal and light up our cigarettes when who should walk in but the swaggering team from British Paints. They were the last people we wanted to see, given the mission we were on. They spotted us and in no time at all the game of one-upmanship started. "Sales" is a mean territory to battle on – there is camaraderie on the surface but cold murder underneath. In every Corporate House, Sales is the most hated department even though it generates everyone's salary, simply because it is made up of men who look mean and menacing. The reason for this physical deformity is simple. Sales personnel engage in war every day of their lives in the field.

And so it was that on that mid-morning in Champapur's Mamta Hotel, a war was afoot. The conversation went something like this.

(BP stands for the enemy and M stands for my colleague, Manoj)

BP – Going where?

M – Not going, returning.

BP – From where?

M – (Laughs a dry laugh & winks a sweet wink).

BP – What?

M – Don't play games with Uncle.

BP – (Looking nonplussed) No really yar! Returning from where?

M – (Rolling his eyes) Okay bête, if you are so desperate to rub it in, then YES, we are returning from the Barauni Oil Refinery. YES we were camping there uselessly for their orders. YES, they are placing their orders on you. And YES, Uncle knows that you guys are going there to collect the same. So YES, Congratulations! Now be a sport and pay for our bill! *Itna toh banta hai*!

BP – (Exchanging confused looks.) What?

M – *Abbe baith na harr baat mein "what"*!

BP – (Exchanging whispers now and appearing to arrive at an agreement) – *Nahi yar*, we had just stopped by for water. Bye, see you.....and see you Mr Sinha.

The British Paints team rushed to their car and sped off to the Barauni Refinery while Manoj and I sat back and laughed at having dispatched the enemy on a wild goose chase. We decided to give them a head-start and then rush to Bhagalpur without any further ado.

We had no idea what lay in wait up ahead.

The two of us got into the back seat and asked our burly driver to get going. In no time at all, we were zipping. The green and brown country side became a blur. The cool air breezed into us, the eyes drooped and our heads started to roll......

BUMP, SCREECH, JUMP, LURCH.... .into this peace-shattering mess, we shot up, startled. In that one instant we knew that our car had run over someone, our driver had jammed the breaks then pressed the accelerator and we were now hurtling forward once again in a frenzy...I looked back and thought I saw something/someone lying in the middle of the road in the furiously receding distance. The driver was jabbering and so was Manoj. I could now see people emerging out of nowhere like ants and running towards us both from behind and front.

STOP STOP STOP we screamed at the driver who now looked completely demented. He was heading straight for the mob which stood not more than thirty meters ahead with what looked like staves and bricks......

He did slow down but still tried to plough through the people who were baying for our blood and pummeling our car with lathi blows and stones. Our windows, which we had rolled up hurriedly, were shattered. One hand reached through the driver's side and smashed a huge piece rock of on his head. By reflex I raised my saddle-brown brief case as a shield for my head while rocks and stones rained over us. The car lost direction and speed. Our driver slumped onto the steering wheel, his head in a bloody mess. There was a grassy embankment – we rolled down it and finally came to a juddering stop.

Heart beating wildly, I struggled out of the partially toppled Ambassador. Trembling with fear I joined my hands to seek mercy from the mob leering down at us from a height of about ten feet.

Have you ever faced a hostile mob? I hope you have not and never will because it has madness in its eyes and blood on its tongue. It closes in on you with the glee and saliva of the executioner. It pulsates with revenge and it is possessed with just one intent – to stamp you out.

I struggled up the grassy embankment, my knees quaking. This was it I thought looking behind and below me, searching for Manoj. There was just the fallen car and the driver's lifeless arm hanging out of a window.

Those who surrounded me were snarling men who taunted me for gallivanting around in a "tuxxie". For some unfathomable reason, they seemed to hold back. While I was being pushed around and toyed with, I kept saying something but I can't recall what. What I clearly recall is that I was in that state of indignity that only total fear can induce....

Just then a jeep arrived on the scene – people turned their heads. A tall and muscular man stepped out followed by another toughie. He walked up to me and asked me what had happened. I told him what I knew, the words tumbling out of my mouth faster than my thoughts. He nodded and looked down at the wrecked car. Then he asked his lackey to bring the driver up. I stood and watched with the assembled villagers who had gone strangely quiet. Just as the driver was being eased out, the rear door opened and Manoj stepped out....

Five or ten minutes later we were speeding away in the jeep towards the Nazareth Hospital in Mokameh which fortunately was just half an hour away. We were bundled in the back seat. The driver was alive but bloodied and unconscious. His head was an absolute mess. It transpired that the only reason we had not been lynched was because the child that our car had run over had been saved – in fact she was not even seriously injured....Gradually I started to breathe evenly and took stock of the situation. Just then Manoj nudged me and pointed to the floor of the jeep. There were half a dozen rifles there....

We became cautiously curious and learnt that our benefactor was a well known civil contractor of the area. Instantly Manoj perked up and became curious. Having established what kind of work the man did, he handed our visiting cards to him and told him that if ever he needed paints, we were the right people to come to at Patna. I glared at Manoj. In return he made a gesture of reassurance and gave me his exasperating Buddha smile.

We reached the hospital in record time. As soon as the injured driver was pulled out of the jeep, the contractor nodded to us and sped off. I asked Manoj to take a train to Patna immediately (the Mokameh station fortunately was so near, we could even see it from where we were) and bring the driver's family back with him in another vehicle – we had hired our taxi from the taxi stand at Patna Station and so it would be easy for him to locate the family. "I will stay here till you return," I told him. "Come back fast."

They asked me many questions in the Emergency Ward but I was quite composed by then. The injured man was in bad shape and would have to be operated upon immediately. I probably signed some papers too, I am not sure….There continues to be partial amnesia.

But the thing I remember with absolute clarity is the sight of the senseless driver stretched out on a gurney and breathing unevenly - a female nurse standing by me and instructing me to take off his

clothes - me looking at her horrified and repelled –
she walking away briskly and advising me to be
quick.

That has been one of the most selfless things I
have ever had to do in my life. It was not social work,
it was not goodness or humility….it was plain and
simple absence of choice. I peeled his clothes off. I
was careful of course. I was not resentful but neither
was I intoxicated with love for humankind. The
climax of the whole thing was what took the cake.
You see when I came to the basics, I saw to my horror
that our man in question was wearing v-shaped
briefs with flowery prints!

Manoj Chakravarty came back with the driver's
family at around eight in the night. I was exhausted
and famished by then. When I asked him why he
had taken so long, he told me with absolute honesty
that after reaching Patna, he had gone home, taken
a bath, partaken his lunch and thus fortified had
gone about hunting down the dying man's family.
He actually saw nothing amiss in it. That was Manoj,
the ultimate sales colleague!!

P.S.

A fortnight later, there was a sort of commotion in
my office. My cabin door swung open. The contractor,
rifle slung across his shoulder, barged in. He literally
flung a bundle of notes on my table and making
himself comfortable, asked for a cup of tea. He then
placed a large order on us. The biggest single order

billing for Nerolac Paints' Bihar Branch was done by us that day. After he had departed, we counted the notes. Fifty thousand rupees! It was by far the largest sum of money any of us in the office had ever seen in our lives till then. To celebrate, the very informal Manoj took yet another cigarette from my packet. I used to smoke Capstan those days.......

Such then is the type and life of men like me who can look back with nostalgia and say with not a little wonder – I was in Sales!

MIST

Infinite is the song
That spirals in the mist,
Loose ends of winter nights
Live encased in my fist.

This happened during the same phase of my life when I was peddling paints. I was young and happy, the world was young and pretty and hence a numberless room in a nondescript hotel in God-forsaken Muzaffarpur was also cool! I remember it was a cold winter night and I was at a loose end having concluded my business with the biggest retailer in town quite satisfactorily. I decided to go out for a walk and may be find an interesting eatery. I did not quite fancy a greasy dinner in my room at the hotel. I loved walking anyway. I rubbed my hands happily at the prospect of stepping out into the misty night. At times like this I loved my lonesomeness. The hotel was located in a quiet area. Outside, it was quite dark. I buttoned my jacket up to the neck, lit a cigarette and started walking.

I was near a busy intersection and poised to cross, when with a startling rush, a bundle of something broke out of somewhere and dashed into me. Next instant, a small hand was clutching mine. Taken aback I looked down to discover an urchin with bright shiny eyes not more than 3 feet tall, looking up at me and jabbering. He was tugging at my hand and pleading "*Bhaiya, hummar Bhaiya, roadva paar kara deejiye na*". The fierceness with which those small fingers gripped my hand left me with no choice at all. So with an amused expression, I held one thin arm of the child in rags and nodded my head. I waited carefully for the traffic to flag and when I was sure, crossed the road with my ward tightly in my control. No sooner had we crossed and I loosened my grip, that the wiry lad disengaged himself with the same sudden ferocity and was off.

Taken completely off-guard, I could do nothing but stare with astonishment after the fast disappearing bundle of energy. He was singing at the top of his voice and bounding away. I just stood where I was and laughed. No thank-you, no good-bye, no gratitude, no nothing. Just a pure and spiraling song that washed the night clean of all things dirty and artificial.

That incident has remained etched in my mind as if it happened just the other night. I can't help but wonder about that little scoundrel. And I like to believe that he is still somewhere in the mist, singing his happy and unfettered song.

TRAIN TO JALPAIGURI

The unspoken unknown burning bright
With hidden beats that snaked the night,
While on a railway station, Mom
Cooked a meal for my father on
A winter's night of fretful turning
Blank pages of a book of learning.

Honestly speaking, I was not at the table when this dinner was served. But it's so delicious that I wish I was...........

My elder brother was a "planter", meaning he was a Manager on a Tea Estate. And while he managed the estate, my sister-in-law managed their generous abode.

One could not wish for a more idyllic holiday than a visit to a planter's Estate. You would be assigned an airy and high ceilinged room in a sprawling bungalow surrounded by greenery. You would be looked after with meticulous care not only by the host and hostess but by a retinue of staff. You would be served elaborate meals punctuated by *nimbu-pani*, coffee, gin, beer…name it and it would "materialize"! Not too many miles away, there would be a club with tennis courts, swimming pool, billiards room and a busy lively bar, the proverbial "watering hole" for planters from all neighbouring estates to gather and gossip. The drive would be through verdant valleys and at the edge of it all there would probably be a forest with wild beast of all kinds. At night, cozy in your warm and quilted bed, if you were lucky, you would even hear the distant "aa-oonh" of the Royal Bengal tiger and your nights, like your days, would burn bright with an unspoken unknown that shimmers across all tea estates…… and while we, the blissfully ignorant visitors sipped our beverages, professionals like my brother who actually managed these estates, dealt with these surreptitiously snaking & loping menaces day-in & day-out with their unique management expertise of man, beast and machine….

For Planters there was another downside. Distanced thus from city life by layers of remoteness, they had no choice but to send their children away for schooling from the earliest stages. And so it was that my niece, Natasha, lived and schooled in Patna in her early years, under the care of my doting parents.

December of 1989, the Notre Dame Academy at Patna closed for the winter. Late one night, my parents along with little Natasha, boarded the North East Express. Their destination: Jalpaiguri. My brother and sister-in-law would pick them up from there and drive the many miles to the Central Dooars Tea Estate where my brother was the Manager. The train journey, crossing over from Bihar into Bengal and moving slowly into the undulating stretches of the Dooars before creeping into Assam, would be a long one. And in keeping with the aura surrounding those tea estates, it would also be a unique one if you were actually headed for one of them.

The following day, when the train was near the Bihar-Bengal border, it slowed down considerably before jerking into a pattern of halts, fits and starts. Word came around that there had been an accident further down the line. Anxious enquiries yielded very little by way of concrete information. The train finally came to a definitive halt at Kishangunj station. The harried guard told my father, "...*kuchh nahi keh sakte sa'ab. Aage accident hua hai. Abhi toh time lagega.*"

The scheduled time for reaching Jalpaiguri was 9 p.m. Dinner was planned to be had in my brother's car on the drive back to the Estate. Everything had been planned with excitement and my sister-in-law, excellent cook, had *seekh-kabab, paratha* and *phirni* in mind. In finicky contrast, my brother had paper tissues, cloth napkins, spoons, forks and glasses, on *his* mind!

Kishangunj used to be a very quiet, nondescript station. As the hours ticked by and the initial thrust and sound of curious passengers lapsed into fretful lethargy, the motionless train sighed itself seamlessly into the darkening country side. The couple of food vendors quickly ran out of stock and the Station Master, having earlier informed that *"train jab khulegi tab khulegi"*, quietly bolted the door of his office from inside and went to sleep.

Hunger pangs started to bother my two and a half strong family after some time. They had run out of the food they had started the journey with, never anticipating that with dinner time approaching they would still be stranded at the dimly lit Kishangunj station. Around 7 p.m., with no new sign or news of any sort, my mother decided that she must scour the platform to see if she could get hold of some food. Hence she and Natasha stepped out. Choosing to remain in his seat was my father, sullenly wordless, not complaining but radiating many shades of disquiet.

My mother had not gone too far when she spotted an enterprising vendor, who had apparently restocked his stall, anticipating that dinner time was fast approaching and there would be a sudden spurt in demand for food. The intelligent fellow understood the value of "fast food" in the circumstances and was all set to sell *dosas* and *samosas.*

I must now tell you a bit more about my father. Even though he was a very progressive and broad minded man, in the context of food he was hopelessly and embarrassingly "narrow". To illustrate - on one occasion he had famously complained that at a banquet he had attended, there was no *dal* to go with the *biryani* that had been served!!

My poor mother therefore knew that even though the *dosa* and *samosa* would do quite well for her and her grand-daughter, neither would find favour with her husband. So she quietly explained her problem to the food seller and made a request. He threw up his hands and informed my mother that he did not know how to make *poories*. So my mother asked if he would be kind enough to allow her to use his raw materials and cooking facilities. He was incredulous but he was both curious and kind. They settled for a price.

And so, at 7 pm thereabouts, on a cold, draughty, darkening night in December of 1989, my mother rolled a few balls of flour, fried a few *poories* and rustled up a quick *aloo-tarkari* for her husband at a food seller's make-shift stall on a way-side railway platform! While this enterprise was taking place, my totally oblivious father was probably checking his watch once again – this time not to see how late the train was but to wonder what his wife and grand daughter were up to for so long!

My parents' life is a book of learning that may never get written. But this much I will say with certainty - their married life was touched by no less than the hand of God.

FINDING SAMMA

Came a season ending all seasons,
Went a brother over the wall,
A forever-house one could reason
Would find echoes if nothing at all,
Vulnerable slants in name and shoulder,
Grey haired men looking so much older,
Like driftwood they met, the sun was bleeding,
Remains of the day were fast receding.

If fathers tend to discuss matters of gravity with their eldest sons and mothers look out for their youngest with extra concern, then I was the middle son!

If, out of a group of five boys, the top two rejected me and the younger two walked hastily away, then I was the odd center who had to learn to fend for himself!

If H & S had bicycles and V & Y had tricycles, then I learnt the art of staying firmly on my feet!

And if all the above were as they were, then logically I would be the loneliest and unhappiest boy of all.

LOL, ROFL, FOTHSL! NOT AT ALL!

In reality, I was the happiest, the most *bindaas*, the biggest scoundrel of them all. And there were reasons. All said and done, I was always in the embrace of a unique family which taught its children, among so many values, the art of being open to the sky. I was also my *Dadi's* pet, all my uncles and aunts made me their favorite nephew, I had the highest number of nicknames – from the jauntily slanted *"Tirchhe"* to the steeped-in-the-soil *"Rajva"*- and lastly, my "best friend forever" lived just across the road. His name was Shyam Sundar Choudhary Pasi. He was the son of the cycle-repair-*wala*. Everyone called him Samma.

Samma was roughly my age or so I felt. He was small built but with a smile which could light up the entire neighborhood. We hit it off together from very early and he in fact was the sixth member whenever the five of us ganged up together on a common mission.

We played marbles together and *lattu* and *pitto*. We explored every nook and cranny of the unkempt grounds in the middle of which squatted my beloved square shaped home with the square shaped portico. We spent hours in the guava tree, watching the world wheel past on the other side of the boundary wall…. together we grew up from innocent children into girl-obsessed teenagers and sat on the back steps of the house and talked in whispers. Samma was the absolute keeper on my confidences. It's difficult to define my relationship with Samma. Let's just say, he was a brother, no less.

There finally came a season which ended all seasons. I left home. During those college years of my turning into manhood at Calcutta, Samma simply went out of my life. When I came home for holidays, he was not around as he used to be. Even I had other things, other places, other people to engage with. We met occasionally of course, but it was different. The boundary walls were the same but Samma now leaned from the other side.

I got married. I have no recollection whatsoever of Samma's presence during that momentous event of my life. He must certainly have been in the periphery somewhere, but I wasn't looking.......And the years slipped by....

I had started working and was posted at Ahmedabad when the distressingly destabilizing news came that the family at Patna was moving out of the "forever house" on Exhibition Road. It was never my ancestral home as I had believed all these years it was. "We" had lived in that house as tenants for close to half a century and then one day strangers came calling......

But this story is about Samma.

Years later and years ago, I was in Patna for a partial reunion with the scattered family. *Bari Amma* and my parents lived in a spacious 8th floor flat on Fraser Road now. We, several of us, were chatting in the living room. Inevitably we turned nostalgic and old B&W albums started coming out. I went back to my childhood but not as a child. Now I was in my forties and turning prematurely grey. Of a sudden, the passage of time hit me in the gut and I was gasping for air.

Next day, I made some excuse and stepped out. Fraser Road runs parallel to Exhibition Road, so I walked. If you have not guessed already then let me tell you – I had decided to find Samma. We had not seen each other for roughly 25 years.

There was nothing left of my Exhibition Road home as I stood and stared. Nothing. Not even an inch of space through which I could grab an echo from the years gone by. I looked at the dirty, untidy structures that now mocked me and felt utterly defeated. How could I find Samma in such an alien place? I looked around and then started walking down the old road, feeling helpless and foolish. I stopped at a tea stall and asked the few men sitting around if they knew Samma – Shyam – Shyam Sundar Choudhary. They shook their heads. At another place of enquiry, someone asked me why. With hope surging, I said Samma was my friend. He too shook his head.

I went about my mission painstakingly on both sides of Exhibition Road. By now people were even staring at me and whispering. I was back to where my old home used to be and standing irresolutely, when someone tapped me. He asked me if I was the one looking for Shyam *mistri*.

He told me that there was a Shyam Scooter Center on Bhattacharya Road. Bhattacharya Road meets Exhibition Road at the crossing where I stood, so I quickly thanked my kind informant and crossed over into Bhattacharya Road. After about twenty minutes of enquiry, I entered a by-lane. I had hardly gone fifty meters, when I saw the battered sign which read "Shaym Scooter". Even though he was bent over a prone two-wheeler, I knew, from the vulnerable slant of his shoulders, that he was Samma.

I tip toed behind him and in as even a voice as I could manage, said "Shyam Sundar Choudhary Pasi"! He froze and then when you would have been least prepared, he uncoiled and spun around with the speed of lightning. This was vintage Samma. His hand flew to his mouth. "Raj *Babu*" he whispered…. his eyes wide with disbelief.

Two grey-haired men in their forties, staring at each other and embracing and the years melting away……

Samma took me to his home – he was keen that I should meet his *"pairvaar"*. From the by-lane we turned into a warren of narrow stone passages and before I knew it, he led me through an open door and into his home…….Samma made his several children come and touch my feet as I sat on a wooden *chauki*. I protested but he insisted. His eldest son, a teenager, looked sullen. When he came forward, I stood up and shook his hands. I feigned a punch in his solar-plexus and told him that his father and I were buddies when we were his age. I saw then that he had his father's smile.......I was keen to see Samma's wife but she remained resolutely hidden behind the *aanchal* of her saree.

I must have had tea and snacks in Samma's home. I don't remember. It was dark in there. And then it was time for me to go. I took my leave and stepped out. Samma came with me. The remains of the day were fast receding. I took out some currency notes from my wallet and gave them to Samma. Without a moment's hesitation he took them and without looking he kept them in his pocket. He was smiling at me and I was searching his face...

Those were the final signatures on our relationship – a clumsy attempt on my part to give a monetary shape to something priceless and on his part, to its graceful smoothening by sheer humility. Both of us knew we would never be seeing each other again. We just knew.

Sometimes it's best to simply let go. Did we not admire the driftwood sailing past? Haven't we known that real beauty lies in its very imperfection?

BROKEN SPARROW

What is it about summers
That takes me back to the dusty past,
The guava trees, the yellowed grass,
A faceless window, stark and bare;
I looked backwards into the cornice,
But the sparrow wasn't there.

O ur house on Exhibition Road at Patna, the one
with the famous garage (which almost got burnt
down once) had a row of outhouses. You stepped out
of our home, went down the porch steps, looked left,
and there, beyond the curving stone-strewn drive-
way, were these three tiled outhouses with a common
cemented façade distempered in white. Two well
spaced doors, one after the other, opened into two
separate rooms, while the third door, a massive set
made of tin-sheets nailed on wooden frames, opened
into the garage. This unit of our multi-faceted home
got even more sharply defined by two walls that
jutted out like two robed arms on either side of the
outhouses. These walls defined the dimension of

the *chabootra* that spread outwards from the base of the outhouses like a gray carpet.

I have attempted to describe the above in detail because a great deal of our childhood was spent here. And this happened largely because of Tiwary-ji.

His full name was Shankar Dhari Tiwary. He was a young, strongly built, fair skinned man, with hair so closely cropped that it did not need combing. Of medium height, he had soft brown eyes and a moustache so standard it was almost inevitable on his old-world visage. He always wore *dhoti-kurta* at home but when he went to the Patna Law College where he was a student, he wore trousers and shirt. He was the nephew of our family *'purohit'*, the old and original Tiwary-ji who now lived in his village and visited us once or twice a year. We always looked forward to his visit on *Makar Sankranti* – the *dahi* he brought from the village was better than any ice-cream you have ever had.

Our "Tiwary-ji" (the young Shankar Dhari Tiwary) was, as per modern day definitions, our guest. He lived in the room on the extreme left as you stood facing the outhouses and his meals were either served to him there or in the *purana chauka* (old kitchen). The *purana chauka* was set in back of our home as a unit separate from the main house, just like the outhouses. Its barracks-like *kothris* with a long smooth verandah running alongside had been inexplicably abandoned by the family sometime in my infancy.

Tiwaryji's arrival at Exhibition Road I have no recollection of. He was just there like happiness is just there in nostalgia. He was a very warm and nice person who we took to with the ease and naturalness of the breeze on our upturned faces.

He participated in almost all aspects of our life in some unobtrusive way or the other. For example, he played *lukka-chori* and *pitto* with us, chaperoned us to the rare movie on the request of elders, told us tales from the Ramayan and Mahabharat, gave us glimpses into village life....once when his college mate (the son of the IG of Police, no less) had left after visiting him in his modest abode, he asked us if we had learnt anything from Devendra's humility....and most memorable of all, when we ran to him excitedly with our report cards, he used to laugh with happiness, clap his hands and exclaim "thank you, thank you"!!.

On many an afternoon we sat around him on the verandah of the *purana chauka* while he ate his meal of rice, *dal, tarkari* and *achaar.* He had such an engaging way of eating that we always ended up feeling hungry no matter how full our stomachs were. He would sprinkle water around his shiny brass *thali*, create a well in his mound of rice and pour the *dal* in it. He would also insert a green chili in the rice. Fascinated, we would watch him eat, waiting for the moment when the *dal* would breach the white embankment....He used to talk to us and we used to talk to him – child stuff, dream stuff, village stuff, city stuff....they were wonderful conversations that flowed with natural ease and on occasions even meandered into his cool and dimly-lit room.

One day, much to our consternation, we found a stranger sleeping in Tiwaryji's bed. Incensed, we asked him where Tiwaryji was and even more demandingly, who he was and what he was doing in Tiwaryji's room. The stranger exclaimed, "Oh you mean Shankar?' and laughed. He sat up, smiled at us and informed us that Shankar was his younger brother. "I have sent him somewhere but don't worry he will be back soon." We glared at the stranger, disliking him even more for referring so rudely to Tiwaryji as Shankar. He was small built, dark complexioned and looked like a rat. He didn't look like Tiwaryji from any angle and we didn't like him one bit.

The man turned out to be Tiwaryji's cousin, a distant one at that thank God. He was in the city, looking for a job. Over the next few days we came to accept him, albeit reluctantly – however even I was old enough to notice that Tiwaryji , though younger, admonished this guy frequently and kept asking him why he was spending so much time idling. But idle he did and quickly got us hooked to his descriptions of village belles and their wayward ways. He took care to tell us his stories only when we were alone with him. In turn we knew by instinct that Tiwaryji was not to be taken into confidence. The rat I am sure understood our instincts too.

All this must have happened during one of our long holidays because we had got into an exciting routine of sorts. Our story sessions were now being addictively held in the quiet of Tiwaryji's room post lunch when the rest of the world had withdrawn into itself and left us to our shades and shadows of whispered tales.

I think Tiwaryji sensed that something was amiss. One day, we were midway into the story of 'The Insatiable Widow' when Tiwaryji barged into the room. We were taken completely off guard. We hadn't heard him or his bicycle. He was not expected for at least a couple of hours for such was his weekday routine of college, library, friends, errands and all. We could see he was angry. He asked us in a very quiet voice to leave. We had never seen Tiwaryiji in such a commanding light so without a word all of us filed out of the room. Tiwaryji had closed the door after we left but we could hear him speaking angrily to his cousin. We hung around for a while and then on the advice of *Bhaiya* slinked away raggedly into the silent and cavernous afternoon.

We never saw the rat again.

I have this regret which I will carry into my dust – that as children we never visited a village. I wish I had spent at least one winter night lying in a barn on stacks of hay, warm and cozy under a rough blanket made from shoddy wool, the cold dark night pocked outside by the light of stray lanterns and animal calls. Tiwaryji would listen to us with a smile and promise to take us to his village in the coming winter. He did nothing to puncture those happy images in our minds and who knows, they may not have been so ill-conceived after all!

Well such a winter never came – they never do.

But a season came, as it always does, when the wind dropped, the flower wilted and the sparrow broke away.

Tiwaryji left us. He got a job - with Defense Accounts. Strangely his departure (to Siliguri) is blank in my memory barring the image of his coming up to *Dadi's* verandah and touching her feet to seek her blessings before leaving.

As the years rolled by and we grew up, the family moved out of the forever-house on Exhibition Road. One after the other, most of us even left the city of our birth. Life took its toll in more cleaving ways too till we, the Exhibition Road boys, were left bewildered and wondering, (now regrouped in depleted numbers at Patna as greyimg, middle aged men), where and when we had left our childhood behind.

Bari Amma had passed away and we were at the Lala Lajpatrai Memorial Hall for a prayer meeting. Her passing had been notified in the local edition of The Times with her photograph, picked by us from the several we had of our beloved elder. The proceedings were about to start when I noticed an old man with a thatch of white hair, shuffling into the hall, looking hesitantly here and there, his hands joined together. My heart skipped for I recognized Tiwaryji instantly. I walked up swiftly to him, held his hands and told him who I was. He looked at me, his memory triumphing over the cobwebs. "Raj Babu" he whispered. He gripped my hands firmly and told me he had got to know from the newspaper......I remember breaking down and telling him that *Bhaiya* was no more....that shook him because we had been his children once upon a time....

After the prayers Tiwaryji, old and infirm, met each member of the family one by one with tears in his eyes. The four of us ('boys') helped him to the rickshaw that would take him to his abode, wherever that was (he lived with his son now). He did not even have a phone number which he could share with us. Life had clearly passed him by.

As children we did not have a life time to look back on to be able to filter the gold from the dust. But as I watched Tiwaryji's rickshaw move away, I realized that he had actually been our first teacher. Not in the scholastic sense, not at all. We never went to him for solving our sums or correcting our grammar....never. What he taught us he did without his telling and without our knowing. For isn't that how we learn about goodness?

Flower With A Spine

The corporate road
Of bending, scraping, skipping and tagging;
The silken routes
That always entice and end up gagging:
I moved nonetheless on a frozen wave,
With the help of hands that reached and saved.
And thus in the rain there was blessed sunshine,
Just like in a flat-bed, a flower with a spine.

The "Corporate" road is a tedious, devious and bumpy road to travel on. There are those who skillfully navigate through its many twists and turns with in-born/acquired finesse and competence. Others learn the art of bending, scraping, skipping and tagging, of finding silken routes under the treacherous mine-fields and in so doing, cover envious distances. And there are the many like me, who struggle through the bewildering maze of passages with mediocrity and finally fall or step off, bruised, unaccountably bewildered and sometimes belittled!

It can be a moronic road too. I want to share two good examples.

The first one is about my first boss. He got very agitated when I was rewarded with certain levels of responsibility very early in my career. I overheard him complaining to Headquarters over the trunk line – *"Yes sir, but I am an MBA too, only the B is missing!"* Later events seemed to indicate that just as I had overheard him through the common partition between his cabin and mine, he too had overheard me laughing out loud!

Many years later, in a different company, during a review meeting, when the assembled managers were asked, turn by turn, to expand on *"I had not thought...."* to articulate what had gone wrong during the preceding year, I looked at the CEO when my turn came and said, *"socha na tha ke itne saare meetings honge aur kaam ke liye itna thoda waqt milega!"* I leave it to you to judge who clearly was the moron in this instance!!

But this slice from my life is not a maudlin or hilarious narrative about my career – far from it. In reality, it is about the unconventional trophies that I won along the way. It's about the joy, love and respect that I was so fortunate to receive.

In this regard just one incident is more than enough to covey the most long-lasting and happy aspects of my career.

There came a time in my career when I was faced with an absolute impasse, an utterly untenable position. It led to my falling horribly foul with the powers that be and so one day I was shown the door with a rude gesture. The situation got so soured and the style of management became so whimsical, that during the limited number of days I was allowed to get into an alternative employment, I was made an outcast. During the unavoidable occasions when I had to step out of my cabin, the heads behind the many desks and desk-tops in the general hall, ducked in one well synchronized downward and frozen Mexican wave. The fear of getting positively associated with me was so pandemic that I was denied even the friendly acknowledgment of an eye contact! My secretary went to the extent of making excuses about being over-worked when I asked her to update my CV to help me send job applications elsewhere. I was a pariah and I knew it.

One day, during this phase, someone knocked on my glass door. I looked up to find a junior colleague wanting my permission to enter. Surprised I nodded and gave a weak, unsure smile. I noticed then that she carried in her hand a napkin covered saucer.

"Sir, it's my birthday. There was a cake cutting ceremony in the hall. I have brought a piece of the cake for you. I have come to seek your blessings."

I got up, shook her hands, wished her well and with a great deal of uncertainty nodded my head when she asked me if she could sit down. I felt responsible for her well being so I asked her if she was sure she should have walked in so openly into my cabin, that too with a smile and a piece of chocolate cake! She used a dismissive gesture at that (understanding fully what I meant) and I was struck by her utter disdain for the shock that I knew was spreading outside like an infection. Her courage and self-assurance belied her young shoulders.

From then onwards, she visited me frequently and helped me in whatever manner she could. Finally the day and moment arrived when it was time for me to walk out of my lonely and forsaken cabin for good. My young friend was with me of course to escort me out. I hate formal or elaborate send-offs and farewells – it's in my nature to slink away (or to be easier on myself), to fade out. But she insisted on walking the long corridors alongside me right up to the car park. She had a way about her which was both authoritative and affectionate, an engaging manner to which it was so nice and comfortable to submit.

Just before I drove out of the parking lot, my young friend, no longer my colleague, gave me a tall flower, a solitary rose. I thanked her and blessed her. I glanced once in the rear view mirror. She was standing erect, watching me drive away. She reminded me of the farewell gift she had given me – she made me think of a flower with a spine.

There are many snippets, many faces. All unforgettable. When I see them smiling back at me, clear as sunshine in the rains, I am left with a sense of unfathomable humility and an enduring faith in the goodness that flows through the veins of some people.

About the author

Born and brought up in a large middle class family, Raj Sinha completed his school education from St.Xavier's, Patna. He then graduated in Economics from St.Xavier's College, Kolkata before completing his post graduation in Business Management from XLRI, Jamshedpur.

He began his corporate career with Asian Paints in 1975 and ended the same 38 years later with Bombay Dyeing. For 1 year he also taught Business Management as a fulltime Associate Professor at the Fore School of Management, New Delhi.

After hanging his boots, he has taken up writing as a serious hobby. Broken Sparrow (which in a sense are his memoirs) is his first publication.

He lives in Mumbai with his wife Poonam.